I could feel the game. I could feel everything that was going on. It was as if every player had a string on him and the strings were all tied to me. Anytime anybody moved, I could feel it. I saw everything and knew what everybody was doing. We started coming back. The ball felt good in my hands. When I went up for a shot from the top of the key, it was as if I had never let the ball go, like I was reaching from the top of the key and directing the ball into the hoop.

WALTER DEAN MYERS has written several picture books and young adult novels. Mr. Myers lives in Jersey City.

HOOPS

Walter Dean Myers

Published by
Bantam Doubleday Dell Books for Young Readers
a division of
Bantam Doubleday Dell Publishing Group, Inc.
1540 Broadway
New York, New York 10036

Based on an original screenplay by John Ballard with additional material
by Dennis Watlington.

Lyrics from "Your Feet's Too Big" by Ada Benson & Fred Fisher:
© 1935, 1936 by Edwin H. Morris & Company, a division of MPL
Communications, Inc. © renewed 1963, 1964 Morley Music Co.
International copyright secured. All rights reserved. Used by permission.

Lyrics from "Rich Land Woman" by John Hurt: Copyright 1963
Wynwood Music Co., Inc. All rights reserved. Used by permission.

ISBN: 0-440-93884-8

RL: 4.7

Reprinted by arrangement with Delacorte Press

Printed in the United States of America

April 1983

OPM 40 39 38 37 36

To my father,
Herbert Dean,
who bought my first
typewriter for me

HOOPS

1

One of the things my father used to say was how his days were piling up on him. When I told him I didn't know what that meant, he said one day I would.

"Right now," he said, "you got your days filled up with playing and going to school. Then after a while you gonna start dreaming about this and that, and you gonna lay your days out in front of yourself like an imaginary road. That's what I did."

"Then what happened?" I asked.

"Then they started piling up on me," he said. He looked away and didn't say anything else, and I knew the conversation was over. When he looked away like that, there wasn't any use to keep on talking.

After he split, I stayed around the house a lot. I did most of the things I was supposed to do, like making the school scene and helping out around the house. I got a little job at the Grant, a little run-down hotel, when I got to be sixteen. That was really okay. I could earn a few bucks, and I could crash there when my moms got on my back too much. By my senior year she was on my back just about all the time, too. Something had come up between us that put an edge on everything we did. It wasn't anything I could really lay out and say, "Hey, there it is," as much as it was a feeling. I'd be sitting in the kitchen eating and she'd come in and make some remark about how late I was staying out or something, and I just wouldn't want to hear it. So I'd finish eating as soon as I could and then bust over to the Grant to spend the night there and cool out.

When I thought about it, I knew it wasn't so much that I had changed, or even that she had changed, but the situation was different than it had been, and we couldn't talk about it. When I was younger, I used to tell myself I was going to do this or do that and I believed it. Now I didn't know. For a long time Moms hung on to that old stuff, about me going to college and making something of myself. When I would lay in bed at the Grant, waiting for the next day to roll around, I was also waiting for something to happen, something to change my life. It was like I was running in a marathon and suddenly forgot where the finish line was. But I knew I still had a place to get to, even if I couldn't see it, and I knew I was scared to stop running.

* * *

All along, though, I had my game. My game was my fame, and I knew *it* was together. From the first time I played basketball in grade school I was good. I was good, but I was short then. Some of the older guys used to call me runt. "You got a sweet game for a kid, runt," they'd say.

I was always on the court practicing, trying to get my game more together. I used to imagine being the shortest guy in the NBA and scoring the winning basket in the championship.

Then, when I got to be fifteen, I started to grow. When my seventeenth birthday came around, I was six three. Now, my game was sweet when I was short, but when I got taller, it was really nice. I played ball just about every day for about three years straight until near the end of my senior year. Then, all of a sudden, I began to go through a whole lot of changes. I was feeling okay, but I just didn't want to do anything. I'd sit around and try to decide what I wanted to do, and that would take an hour or so, and then, when I decided what I wanted to do, I still might not do it because I just didn't seem to have the energy. Then, to top things off, sometimes if I did really break out into a hustle and do something, it would get messed up. I wasn't sure it was me or if things just weren't going my way. The Scotch is a good example of what I mean.

I had had some words with my moms after I had left a tea bag in the sink.

"What's the matter?" she said with her hands on

her hips. "Your arm so bad off you can't reach over there and put the tea bag in the garbage?"

I didn't say nothing.

"You know that tea bag is going to leave a stain and you're not going to clean it."

"I'll put it in the garbage," I said.

"Oh, no, Mr. Jackson," she said in this high voice. "Please let your servant do it."

Then she snatched up the tea bag and put it in the garbage.

"So why didn't you just do that in the first place?" I asked.

"Why didn't I do that in the first place?" She bent over from the waist and looked up at me. "Who do you think I am, boy? I'm your mother, not your servant!"

I listened to that until she got tired of running it; then I split on over to the Grant. I couldn't believe all that flap over a tea bag. I was pretty mad by the time I got to the hotel. I got the keys and went up into one of the empty rooms on the third floor and just sat in the window. I looked over towards the liquor store to see if I could see the clock. I couldn't, and I started to turn away. But something wasn't right. When I looked again, I could see the guy that ran the store standing close up against the shelves, and the clerk was standing right next to him. It looked like there were two other guys in there, too. One of them was a guy who delivered liquor to the store, and the other guy I didn't recognize, but I saw he had his hand in his jacket pocket. That's when I realized the store was being held up.

4

Hoops

Now the truck with the booze to be delivered is outside in the street and the driver is inside being stuck up, which gave me an idea. I busted down the stairs and into the street. I look into the liquor store, and I see that the guy with his hand in his pocket and a third guy I hadn't seen from the window are making everybody go into the back. I go over to the truck, open the back, and there's a case of Johnnie Walker close enough to grab. I look around to see if anybody is checking me out, but the only people on the block are some kids. I cop the case of Scotch and hightail it back into the Grant and up to my room.

I figure I can get at least five dollars a bottle for the Scotch, and there are twelve bottles to a case. I'm feeling pretty good about the whole thing by the time I get the case under the bed. I go back to the window. There's this young brother up on the truck, and I figure he's going to cop, too. But instead of copping a case of something like I did, he takes a padlock off the truck and throws it to another kid. This kid runs up to the liquor store and puts the padlock on the door.

One of the guys inside the store sees what is going on and runs over to the door, but it's too late. The kid has locked them all inside. Then about four or five other kids start unloading the truck. Meanwhile, the guys inside the store are banging on the window and hopping up and down and stuff. By this time it seems that half of Harlem is in on the action. One wino opens a bottle and is in the middle of the street, directing traffic. It takes about ten minutes to unload the truck. The whole block turns into a big party. Finally the cats inside the store shoot out the window just as a police car comes around the corner. There are a few shots fired, but nobody gets hurt, and soon everything is back to normal except for the glass on the street.

It was funny to watch, but then I realized that everybody on the block had Scotch and everything else now, and I wouldn't get nothing for mine. Still, I figured I could lay with it until everybody had drank theirs up. But that was the way my luck was running—even things that looked sweet weren't working out right for me.

I got depressed about the whole thing. I sat in the window and watched the people down in the street having a good time, and I began to feel worse and worse.

I have a funny way of thinking—at least I think it's funny because I don't hear anybody else saying they think the way I do. What I do is to think things part of the way out, and then I put them aside and think them out some more later on. I had begun to think about what my father had said a long time ago about your days piling up on you, and as I sat in the window of the Grant, I began thinking about it again. It was beginning to make more sense to me.

School was going to be out in another five or six weeks, and then I was going to have to figure out something to do with myself. Before, I'd spend the summer playing ball and waiting around until school started again, so that would take care of itself. But now that school was just about over for me, the days seemed different, and I had to figure out what I was going to do with them. I knew I didn't want to work at the Grant all the time. I hated Jimmy Harrison, the manager, and the job was a chump job anyway—sweeping floors and changing beds and that kind of thing. The only thing that made it not so bad was me telling myself it was just until I finished school. I saw a lot of guys who had either finished school or had dropped out just hanging around the block, and I didn't want to do that either. I wondered if my days were piling up on me, like my father said they might. They were changing, at least, or maybe I was changing. Or was supposed to be and wasn't.

I sat in the window for a long time, and then I laid across the bed, just waiting for time to pass. I dozed off for a while, and when I woke, it was just about dark. I thought about going to a movie but decided to save my money so I could go the next day in case it rained. I got a basketball I kept at the Grant and wandered over to the playground. The lights were on, and I figured I'd shoot a few baskets. Playing ball, even shooting baskets by myself, always made me feel better. I figured to shoot until I got tired and then come back and get some sleep.

I had my head so wrapped up in myself I didn't see this guy laying on the court until I got right up on him.

"Hey, man." I nudged him with the toe of my sneaker. "Get off the court!"

When he didn't move, I thought he might be dead. I nudged him again.

"Your feet too big . . ." That's what he said, only he kind of sung it instead of talking.

"Hey, man, get up!"

"I really hate you 'cause your feet too big . . ."

The cat is laying there singing some kind of weird song. I pushed him with my sneaker again, and he didn't move. So I gave him a kick on the back of his leg and told him to move again. He rolled over and got up on his knees and hands like a boxer trying to beat the count. I thought he was getting right up, but he just stayed like that for a while. I reached down and grabbed him by the collar and started to drag him off the court, and then, all of a sudden, he's up. Not only is he up, but he's got this blade in my face!

I dropped the ball and backed off. This guy smells like somebody done peed in bad wine and washed his teeth in it, but he's got this knife, and he's bigger than me.

"Hey, why don't you get off the court, man?" I said.

"I really hates you 'cause your *feets* too big . . ." He starts in with this singing again, and I just watched him. I didn't want to get too close to him 'cause I still didn't know where he got the knife from and he was quick.

He stops just before he gets off the court and turns back to me and just looks at me, and then he puts his knife away. Right away I feel like busting his jaw. I take a step toward him, and he just grins at me.

"Get off the court, old man, before I hit you!"

"Why don't you put me off the court, youngblood?" he says, still grinning.

I look at him for a minute, and he don't look like much. But I'm six three and he's maybe six four, and he's heavier. I wasn't scared of the cat, but I figured it wasn't worth my while. I could hit him and he'd have a heart attack and die and I'd be up for manslaughter or something.

I picked up the ball and shot it. He turned and walked off, still singing that stupid song about feet. I shot a few times, and then the ball came down on something—a broken bottle of wine. I started to push it off the court with my foot, but then I picked it up and threw it off as far as I could. I got the ball again and shot and shot until I was too tired to shoot anymore. Then I took the ball over to the track and ran laps until I could see the sky start turning gray between the buildings.

The next morning Harrison had me cleaning rooms with him and listening to a lot of guff about how hard he had it when he was my age. He'd heard that I was the first to cop from the truck the day before and asked me where I was keeping my stash.

"Don't worry about it," I told him.

He gave me a look hard enough to curdle water and went on sweeping. After we finished cleaning the rooms, I split to Mary-Ann's house.

Mary-Ann is just about my woman. Just about, because I haven't really done anything to make it official.

I've known Mary-Ann and her brother Paul just about all my life. For a long time I treated her like a younger sister. Paul and I were close, too. If I had to call somebody my main man, he'd be it. We were just about the same age and had been going to school together, eating at each other's house and stuff like that for as long as I can remember. Lately Paul had been hanging around with some of the cats at school who thought they were better than the rest of us. This was a new thing with him, and I couldn't figure it, but I gave him the benefit of the doubt.

Mary-Ann was something else. She had been Paul's kid sister and I had liked her, and then one day she just wasn't a kid anymore. I don't know if she just changed or if both of us did. I remember being at Paul's house one day, waiting for him to finish his shower, and Mary-Ann and I were playing checkers. I used to always let her beat me, and then I'd sneak a checker off the table and we'd wrestle around for it. Only this time, when she tried to wrestle me to the floor to get the checker out of my hand, I was suddenly aware that she was a woman. I opened my hand real quick, and she asked me what was wrong, was I getting weak? I just looked at her and she looked at me and we both knew things had changed between us.

I found myself liking her more and more, but I tried to keep it cool. I wasn't really ready for no big love thing, but I liked the way I felt around her, and she knew it, even though I never said it in so many words.

When I got over to Paul's house, he wasn't home. Mary-Ann and her mother were there, mouthing off at each other like they always did.

About six months before, they had been arguing about the fact that Mary-Ann didn't get a new coat for Christmas. Her mother came back with how bad things were and how much this cost and how much that cost and the usual noise people be handing out when they come up short. Then she starts saying that since Mary-Ann had just turned sixteen, she could go out and get her a part-time job or something and help get her own stuff. I guess she figured that Mary-Ann would work in the supermarket or something like that. But there's an after-hours joint across from where Paul lives, and Mary-Ann gets a job there instead.

Mary-Ann's job was to keep track of the liquor and stuff so that the bartenders wouldn't rip off the money from the sales. She ordered stuff like peanuts, and potato chips, too. But her mother kept running down about how Mary-Ann was going to be a tramp because she worked in the after-hours joint, especially when the dude that ran it gave Mary-Ann her own room. Mary-Ann told her mama that the guy wanted her to stay there some of the time so in case he wanted to check things out, she could tell him what was what. Her mama didn't want to hear a thing, so she just kept running the same old lines. Mary-Ann was making about three times as much as she could in the supermarket and she dug the responsibility, so she wasn't about to give up the gig.

After she and her mother had finished putting each other down, we went down and sat on the stoop.

"She just stays on my case," Mary-Ann said. Her eyes were red, and I figured she was ready to cry.

"You know what she's going to say," I said, "so just get used to it."

"I don't dig her always accusing me of 'getting ready to do some dirt,' " Mary-Ann said. "If her stuff

11

wasn't so raggedy, she wouldn't have the dirt on her mind."

"Why I got to hear this?" I asked. "I've heard it a hundred times, and it don't change none."

"Who else I got to say it to?"

"Ease up, mama," I said. "I didn't come to start nothing. I just came over to see what Paul was doing, that's all. Look, you want to catch a flick this afternoon?"

"I got to work," she said. "She always waits until I'm just about out the door before she starts running her mouth."

"All that means I got to go to the flick by myself?"

"You want to see me when I get off work?"

"I'll think about it."

"Jive turkey!" She got up and gave me a smile that made me glad that Paul hadn't been home. I watched her cross the street and head down the block towards the after-hours joint, knowing that she would turn around before she went in. She got all the way to the door and then turned and threw me a kiss. I threw one back underhanded, and she disappeared into the doorway.

I went back over to the Grant to get my sneakers. I had heard that they were looking for some ball-players for some kind of tournament or something. At the Grant there's Harrison sitting behind the desk, writing up a card for some dude and a white chick. The chick wasn't bad. I'm just going to walk on by the desk when I see a bottle of Johnnie Walker Black, half gone, sitting against the wall. So I wait until this cat and his white chick go on upstairs, and I sound on

Harrison. I know that better not be my stuff or I'm going to waste him right then and there.

"Hey, man, you drinking top shelf," I said, pointing to the Johnnie Walker.

"I don't like nothing cheap," he said.

"Well, that ain't cheap," I said. "Wherever you get it from it's going to cost you."

"That right?"

The way he said that I just knew it was my stuff he was drinking. I just *knew* it.

"Look, man, you going to be here long?" I asked. "Because I'm going to go upstairs and check something out, and then I'll be right back down if everything isn't everything."

"Your mama was by here a few minutes ago," he said.

"Say what?"

"I said that your mama was by here a few minutes ago. She said she was sorry to bother you again, but the landlord came and said that she either had to pay the rent or leave the place. I figured since it wasn't that much, I could lend her the money."

I just looked at him and he looked at me. Then he reached over and poured himself another drink. I didn't say anything else. I went on upstairs and looked under the bed and pulled out the box. There were two bottles of Scotch left. When I came down again, I asked him how much he had lent my mama.

"Don't worry about it," he said, "you'll pay it back."

"Hey, look, can I ask you a question?"

"Free country."

"Do you practice being stupid, or is it just natural?"

"Man, that's a real funny joke," he said, leaning back in the chair. "The first time I catch me a free minute I going to sit down and have myself a real good laugh."

I got to the gym, and there's a bunch of guys hanging around. Paul and Ox were there, too, watching some guys playing five-two for quarters. When I get there, the guy who runs the gym, a little West Indian cat, tells Paul to get everybody together. Most of the guys I had been playing with around Harlem most of my life, and I knew they could hoop.

"Okay, you guys are in the tournament," Nesbitt, the West Indian cat, was saying. "Now the tournament consists of two stages. The first stage is to get rid of the scrubs. There are sixty-four teams in the tournament right now."

"Sixty-four teams!" Ox said. Ox is one of these big suckers who looks like Alley Oop. He's about six seven and weighs about two twenty. His game isn't that tough unless he gets mad. Then he gets stronger than skunk pee and can't nobody do anything with him.

"There's sixty-four teams right now," Nesbitt said, "but the way the tournament's set up the weakest teams have to play the strongest first. That way we eliminate the really weak teams up front, but a lot of guys get a chance to play. Now the whole point to the tournament is that there will be college scouts at the games. They're going to be checking out not only how you play but also how you carry yourself."

As Nesbitt went on talking, I noticed somebody come up behind the guys. It was the wino from the park. The first time I saw him face to face in the park I thought I had seen him someplace before, but I couldn't figure where. Now I knew. Sometimes he hung around the gym, watching the guys play ball. Probably to keep warm, I figured, or maybe he was a freak.

"Okay, now Mr. Jones will see to it that you guys get over to the playground tomorrow to play your first game. You'll be playing a team from Staten Island. A guy I know saw them play and didn't think much of them. I want you guys to remember that this is a chance for those of you who didn't play high school ball. Most of the coaches that come will come for the last game or two, which will be held in the Felt Forum if they can get it."

"In the Felt Forum, no lie?" Paul asked.

"That's right."

"Who's Mr. Jones?" I asked.

"This cat." Ox points out the wino.

"You got to be kidding, man," I said. "This cat's a wino. I ain't playing no ball for no wino coach."

"We got to have a coach, and he's the only guy that Nesbitt said was okay," Jo-Jo said. "He said we can't have nobody young for the coach."

"Well, all we need is his name," I said. "Give him some wine and let him find himself a park bench."

"He got to show for the games, too," Ox said.

"Man, we need a coach and he's it," Paul said.

"Hey, look, I done peeped the cat stoned on the ground in the damn playground, man," I said. "What do you say, Ox?"

"I got to consult my bird."

Ox, big as he is, has got this mangy-looking parrot he carries around with him, and I swear he really loves that sucker.

"Hey, Lonnie, I just figured out something," Breeze called out.

"Come on, Ox," I said. "You and me are co-captains."

"Why should you be co-captains?" Paul asked.

" 'Cause we're the best." I said.

"That bird ain't as dumb as I used to think," Breeze went on. "That bird is actually a ventriloquist. Ox is the one who can't talk."

"Okay, then," I said, "it's settled. We ain't playing for no wino. If Nesbitt don't want us in this tournament, we'll find another one."

"Later for you, man!" Paul sounded off on me. Then he walked out of the gym. I ran after him and grabbed him near the door.

"What's with you?" I asked. "I ought to punch you out!"

"Hey, that's what you're good at, ain't you?" He stood against the wall. I still had him by the collar, and I let it go.

"What's the matter with you, man?" I asked. "I saw the man laying on the ground with a bottle of wine so damned drunk he couldn't hardly get up. This is who you want to play for?"

"No, I don't want to play for him, Lonnie," he said. "I want to play for *me*. Dig it? They got college scouts coming to watch these games. Maybe I can get a scholarship or something. Some guys I was talking to were saying that the white schools are always looking for ballplayers. You can get a scholarship to a small white school even if your game ain't together.

All you got to do is have some kind of a game and be cool. What else am I going to do? I can't go to no college on my own."

"What you mean is you want to follow your punk friends to some punk school."

"If it gets me over, yeah."

"Just what won't you do to get over?"

"I'd hate to tell you."

"What does that mean?" I said.

"Nothing. You going to give the guy a chance?"

I didn't answer him. I just went back into the gym. The wino was sitting on the floor putting on a pair of sneakers. I took the ball from Ox and dribbled across the floor and made an easy lay-up.

"Let's play some three-on-three," I said. I had to play some ball. It was the only thing that ever really relaxed me. Some of the other guys took another ball down to the other end of the court and started up a three-man game down there. After the wino had the sneakers on, he started over to where I was but stopped near the top of the key and fumbled around in his pocket until he came up with something he put to his mouth. I thought it was maybe chewing tobacco, but it was a whistle. I couldn't believe it. Here was the wino in the middle of the floor blowing a whistle.

"Hey, why don't you put the whistle away?" Paul said. I had to smile because the wino was taking this seriously, as if he was really going to coach somebody.

"Tell you what I'm going to do," the wino said. "I'm going to play my man here some one-on-one. If he wins, I'll walk out of here and won't say another word. If I win, I'll coach."

"You got to be jiving," I said. "I walked on my share of roaches for the day already."

"You nervous, superstar?" the wino said.

"How would you like me to bust your jaw?" I said, putting my finger to his face.

"Do it with the ball," the wino said, bouncing it to me.

"One-on-one, six baskets."

Some of the guys started moving off the court. I still didn't want to play against no wino, but there I was. I moved down the right side of the lane and just threw the ball up against the backboard. It went in.

"That's one," I said.

"That's one." The wino grinned.

I brought the ball down the left side of the lane and pulled up for a short jumper.

"That's two."

"Go ahead."

I missed the next shot, and the wino got the ball from where it had bounced out of bounds. As he brought it in, I laid back, waiting for him to try to take a shot. He tried a jumper, and I slapped it away. I didn't even try to pick it up. The wino got the ball again, came across the foul line, and made a little move with his shoulder like he was going to try that same jumper again. But as soon as I went up in the air, he went around me.

"That's one," he said.

A couple of the guys started making remarks. I shot them a look and laid back. The wino threw up a jumper from the top of the key. Two apiece.

I still laid back and he threw another jumper from

the top of the key, and it was 3 to 2. He could shoot all right. Maybe he had played some ball once. I got on his case when he came down the side of the lane. He tried to get a step on me, but he couldn't, and when he went up, I was right with him. I pinned the ball against the boards and scooped it down, then hit a turnaround jumper to tie the score, 3 to 3. But he was making it look like it was some kind of real game or something, so I went outside and started a spin on him. I spun outside until I got a half step on him and brought him inside. Then I let him recover from that and put another spin on the sucker on the inside, and then I jammed over him.

I took the ball out again, spun on him on the outside, brought him on inside, and then spun on him again. The first time I had spun to the right, and this time I spun to the left and I laid it in: 5 to 3.

I brought the ball in again, but this time, when I tried the outside spin, he tipped the ball away and recovered. He drove for the basket, and I was on his case about a half step behind him. Then he stopped, and I thought he was going to try for the jumper, but he spun around me and laid it in. There were a couple of oohs and ahs, which ticked me off.

The next time he brought the ball down he went right to the hoop, and I went right with him. I cut him off, or at least I thought I cut him off because I thought he was too deep to make the shot. He was just about behind the backboard. He went up and I went up with him, but then he stretched out and went from the other side and made the lay-up. There were a lot more oohs and ahs.

"Five to five," the chump said.

I didn't say nothing. I threw him the ball and decided that this time he wasn't going to get anywhere near the damn basket. He put the ball on the floor once and threw it up from about twenty-five feet. I turned my back to him and spread my legs to cut him off from the rebound. Only there wasn't any rebound; it was all net as the ball dropped in with a little swishing noise.

"First practice tomorrow at three o'clock!" he said. He had this grin all over his face like he had did something.

"Hey, Mr. Jones," Ox called out, "why you so mean to my man Lonnie?"

"Call me Cal," the wino said.

"Hey, Lonnie, the cat stuffed your game so bad you got to call him *Mr.* Cal," Paul said.

That didn't bother me none. The guy had a little game, but he wasn't that much. If I had been playing the sucker seriously, I would have wiped him off the court. I didn't say anything right then because I didn't want to make no issue of it. But we'd match up again, I knew that. I knew that I would see that we matched up again.

2

They gave us forms to fill out and bring back the next day. I started filling it out at home and got about halfway through before I stopped. They wanted to know how old you were, what year you were in, your grade average, stuff like that. The more I got to thinking about that form, the less I wanted to do with it. What it was all about, the form and the tournament, was copping a plea for a second chance because you didn't make it on the first go-around. That was what Paul was rapping about with his "being cool" jive. I'd peeped that whole show-your-teeth, shuck and jive scene before. Like the time when

I was getting ready to go into junior high school and they were talking about taking kids into this special program. My moms had me going for this interview in a suit and a tie in the middle of May. There was twenty of us sitting in that hot auditorium and going up one by one to talk to these three people who were selecting kids for the special program. A week later we found out that they took the two lightest kids. I wasn't going to dance for nobody, and I wasn't going to hoop for nobody for a chance I probably wasn't going to get anyway.

I didn't hang around with the guys for a while or play any ball. The whole tournament idea got me down. Hey, play ball for the wino and let these scouts dig your game and maybe you can get over. I'd daydream about it. Daydream about me playing my best game and everybody cheering and all the scouts digging my action. But even when I daydreamed, it ended up in the same way: Somebody else got over, and I just had another day to pile up with the rest.

Then one day this cat Cal comes by. I don't know who told him where I was staying unless it was Paul. He come knocking on the door, and I opened, and there he was.

"What you want?" I asked. He didn't say nothing but just came on in and sat down like he owned the place.

"How come you ain't playing with the squad?" he asked.

"What's it to you?" I said.

"I just hate to see a guy with a game as good as yours throw it away," he said.

"I don't need you to tell me how good my game is, you or no other wino."

"You need somebody to tell you how good your game can be," he said. "Because you don't know that."

"Why don't you split, man? When I want to get my team back together, I'll do it."

"How's it your team when you up and cut out on them for nothing?" Cal said. "If that's where you're coming from, they're better off without you."

I don't know what came over me, but I was on him in a minute. I tried to grab him and spin him out the door, but before I knew it, the sucker twisted my arm behind my back and pushed me against the wall. He eased my arm down and asked me, real quietlike, if I wanted to try it again.

"Do me a favor, and just get out of here," I said, trying to get the blood circulating in my arm again. "And don't come back, because the next time I see your face in my doorway, I'm going to blow it away!"

"A friend of mine from the pros is going to be at the practice tomorrow," he said. "Show up if you're man enough."

Then he split. I was really mad. I wanted to punch something so bad I could taste it. Then I remembered the Johnnie Walker Black under the bed. I didn't really dig booze too tough, but it was better than nothing. I took my sneakers off, threw them in the closet, got a glass and washed it out, and went down the hall to the ice machine. I was going to get so drunk I couldn't remember my own name.

I pulled the box out from under the bed. Empty! Harrison had copped the rest of my Scotch. I picked up an ashtray and threw it with all my strength across the room. It hit the drapes and banged into the blinds, but it didn't break. It went under the bed, and I got down on my hands and knees and found it. This time I was about four feet from the wall when I threw it. It shattered into hundreds of pieces that flew all over the room. I cried myself to sleep for the first time since my father split.

There was no way I was going to fall for some jive about no pro coming to a rinky dink gym to watch us practice. I figured that the wino was stringing us along with his bull, and I was just waiting to catch the sucker. I knew he was a phony, but I hadn't peeped his bag yet. He could have been a freak or into some antipoverty scam. Whatever it was, he was being cool with it, but there was no way I was going to trust the dude, no way. Still, I wanted to find out just what he was up to, so I went to the practice. Only I'm not about to put on no sneakers and run around for this dude.

I'm checking him out. He's telling guys how to set picks and how to switch and stuff like that. And he acts like he knows what he's talking about, but that's no big deal because you can pick that up from reading a book. Meanwhile, there ain't no pro showing up. Everybody's running around, listening to this cat Cal like he's their daddy or something and keeping one eye on the door as if God Himself is going to come in any minute, which I figured was about as likely as having any pro come in.

"You going to sit there, or don't you think you're good enough to play this man's game?"

The sucker was on my back again. This dude just kept on pushing and pushing. Sparrow, Ox's parakeet, made a sound, and I asked Cal if he was talking to him. He didn't say anything; he just turned away and kept on with the practice.

He worked out a play, too. I checked the play out and memorized it.

"Okay, now, everybody gather around," Call called out.

They all gathered around.

"I want everybody to come up with fourteen dollars for uniforms," he said. "We're going to get red and green uniforms. I want you to put your money in an envelope. On the outside of the envelope you put your name, your size, and the number you want. Make sure you all have different numbers, too."

"Hey, man, ain't that the Sweet Man?" Ox pointed across the gym, and I turned to see where he was pointing. It was Sweet Man Johnson himself coming towards us. My mouth just dropped open. Except for the bag he had over his shoulder, he looked just like he did on television.

"Hey, I'm sorry I'm late for the practice," he said, "but I had to drop Webster's woman off at a bookstore. Sorry."

Cal introduced everybody to the Sweet Man, and then he said he wanted to see one of the plays again.

Everybody got excited and ran themselves ragged practicing that play. I felt pretty stupid because I didn't have my sneakers. They ran through it about three times before Cal called it a day. Couple of the guys came over and shook hands with the Sweet Man.

"I got to get a cheeseburger," Sweet Man said. "I think it's an emergency."

Cal laughed and asked me if I had time to stop off with them. Naturally I said okay, and we went down the street to a little bar and then got a guy to go out and get the burgers, which was pretty cool. That way Sweet Man didn't have a lot of kids all over him.

"This is the cat you told me had a nice game?" Sweet Man nodded towards me.

"Yeah," Cal said, "Lonnie's pretty nice."

"Glad to meet you, Lonnie." Sweet Man stuck out his hand, and I shook it again. I had shaken it before when Cal first introduced everybody around, but now it was different because it was just me.

"So what you been doing with your bad self?" Cal asked Sweet Man.

"Same old thing," Sweet Man said. "You know I got this record company. I still can't decide about this new group. They got something, you know, they sing good, but . . ."

"I don't know nothing about these pop stars," Cal said.

"You knew enough about them to marry one," Sweet Man said.

Cal looked like he just remembered something he didn't like. It only lasted for an instant, but it was there.

"How'd that other thing we talked about go?" Sweet Man switched the conversation.

"I tried everybody, you know, they don't want to hear nothing."

"How about Lee?" Sweet Man looked at Cal. The

conversation was serious, but I didn't know what they were talking about. I really hadn't figured Cal to know Johnson in the first place. And I sure didn't figure me to be sitting there with the two of them having a cheeseburger. "Look, man, if you're going to get back into the game, you're going to run into these dudes and you're going to run into the same situations."

"Yeah," Cal said. "I guess so."

Then Sweet Man switched the conversation again. He was talking to me, asking me about my game and what I wanted to do with it and things like that, and I just tried to talk it through. When the burgers came, we ate them, and Cal and the Sweet Man started talking about some game they had played in, and from the best I could make out, they had played together. Cal was heavier than I thought he was.

The Sweet Man left soon after we had finished the burgers, and Cal said he had to split. He said there would be a practice the next day, and if I came, I was to make sure I brought my sneakers.

"Look, man." I didn't really know what to say to him. "Thanks for saying I had a nice game."

"I wasn't telling him no lie, Lonnie," Cal said. "You got a nice game, but like he said, you got to be doing something with it."

I could only get eleven dollars together, but Breeze and I both picked the same number, and I let him have it for four dollars, so I had fifteen. Breeze always had a pocketful of money, and Ox said that he thought he was messing with some rich woman downtown, but I didn't believe it.

We practiced hard for the next week and a half, and we were looking good. Cal knew what he was all about, but he was always on my case. It seemed to me that he would tolerate a mistake from anybody except me. If I didn't pass right, he'd stop a play and make me do it over again. If I took a shot when I wasn't supposed to, or if I didn't get through a pick or something, he'd have something to say about it. Everybody else checked it out, too, and it made me feel uncomfortable. I liked what he was doing, and at the same time I didn't like it.

We were supposed to get the uniforms on a Wednesday. Cal announced this at a meeting that I missed because my moms got sick and I had to take her to the hospital. The doctor said it was her pressure, and he gave her a prescription to have filled. I went and got that filled, and by the time I got to the meeting it was over. They had the meeting at Cal's ex-wife's house. He was trying to get back with her. Breeze said that she was only fair, but Ox said she was pretty nice.

"For an older chick she's out of sight, man," Ox said.

"What went down at the meeting?" I asked.

"We will have the uniforms on Wednesday for our first game," Ox said.

"A game?"

"Yeah, we going to play Snakeskin and his boys."

"I thought he was in jail."

"He must have got out if he was because he's going to play us."

"You know what I heard?" Breeze asked. "I heard

that everybody knows about the Sweet Man coming to our practice and about our getting new uniforms and everything! Not only that, but they all coming to the game to see our action!"

"Who told you that?" I asked.

"Everybody's been saying it," Ox said.

"Well, who told them?"

"Us."

Breeze and Ox were both grinning, and I had to grin myself.

The day of the game we were all in the gym early. We ran through a few practice plays, and then we just sat around and talked. We must have done that for about a half hour before Snakeskin's team showed up. Snakeskin, when he wasn't so high he could hardly talk, had a nice game. He was quick in a way that was tricky. Some guys were quick, but they were so herky jerky you were always alert. Snakeskin, on the other hand, was smooth. He'd be moving the ball slow across the top of the key one moment and you'd be moving with him and the next moment he'd be around you, laying the ball against the boards.

Mr. Reese was going to be the referee, and he kept trying to get the game started, but we were stalling, waiting for Cal to show with the uniforms. We had all chipped in and bought a jacket for Cal with "Coach" printed over the pocket, and we figured we'd lay it on him when he brought the uniforms. We kept stalling, waiting for Cal, until Mr. Reese said that we'd either have to start the game or forfeit. So we played in sneakers and whatever we happened to have on.

"They some bad uniforms you got on," Snakeskin said as we lined up for the jump.

"We got them from your mama," I said.

We lost the game by a yard and a half.

When Cal didn't show for the game, we were down, but everybody was trying to keep the team thing together. But when the cat didn't show up the next day either, things got raggedy.

Paul and Jo-Jo went over to Cal's woman's house, and she said she didn't know where he was either. Jo-Jo said that she looked upset but tried to non-chalant it off.

"I think the cat split with the money," Paul said.

"Maybe he got hit by a truck or something." Ox was pouring a bag of peanuts into a Coke.

"When's the last time you seen anybody hit by a truck, man?" Paul asked.

"What you cats talking about?" I asked. "You give up your bread to a wino and then come talking about how he don't show 'cause maybe he got hit by a truck and stuff. If he did get hit by a truck, I hope he's dead."

"How come you so hard on this dude?" Ox was shaking up his peanuts and Coke. "If this dude is such a wino and everything, how come you get so uptight about him?"

"What's that supposed to mean?"

"It's supposed to mean just what the hell it's saying," Ox said. "You done played ball for quarters in the park, you played ball for some cupcakes, and one time you even played ball because that ugly chick who live over the funeral parlor on Lenox said she was going to give some to the winning team. Now all of a sudden you getting uptight because the cat's a wino."

"That don't bother you? The cat rips your butt off and it don't bother you?"

"It bothers me if my bread is gone, but I ain't gonna lose no sleep over it."

"Yeah. Well, that's you. I'm tired of these cats come around and talking like they want to take care of business and don't show when the deal goes down. That's all, I'm just tired of it."

"I don't know, man," Ox said. "Sound to me like you kind of sweet on the dude. How long this been going on?"

"Since I got tired of your mama, sucker!"

"Tell you what I'm going to do," Ox said. "I'm just going to make believe I didn't hear that. Because if I heard it, I'd feel like I just had to break you down like a shotgun, reach up your hind parts, and snatch your heart out. So let's just leave it ride for now. 'Cause if you don't want to leave it, just run it again."

I looked over at Ox and felt like jumping over the table and putting my fist in his face. But I knew what Ox was like when he was mad, stronger than skunk pee and meaner than King Kong's dog, so I left him alone. I just wished anybody else had said it, so I could bust some head.

The center wasn't much, but it was our hangout. It had a gym, but the ceiling was too low for shots from more than twenty feet away. You'd even hit the ceiling from fifteen feet if you didn't flatten out your shot. You could always tell a guy that had learned his ball in the center, because they all had this line-drive jumper. There were four keys to the office. I had one, and Paul, Ox, and Breeze had the other three. We kept records, magazines, extra sneakers, and that kind of stuff in the office. We also had a rusty .32 with a broken handle that we were always threatening each other with. But the thing that made the office special was that Ox kept his parakeet, that he had named Sparrow, there. The parakeet couldn't talk, but we had got into the habit of saying "Hi" to the bird whenever we went into the office. There was a telephone in the office, too, and nobody knew who paid the bill. We figured the center must have been paying for it.

While I was in the center, I got a call from Mary-Ann. She was worried. She said she had been at the after-hours club where she worked and had been in the boss's office and seen this envelope with her brother's name on it.

"Paul's name?" I asked.

"Yeah," she said. "I didn't even know he knew Tyrone."

"Well, so what?" I said. I knew she thought Tyrone, the dude who ran the place, was into the rackets, but I really couldn't figure Paul being involved.

"So I asked Tyrone what he was doing with my brother's name on an envelope and he said that Paul had come and asked him for a job. That don't sound right to me."

"So why you asking me about it?" I asked. "Ask Paul."

"I asked him, and he got all nasty," Mary-Ann said. "Talking about how I should stay out his business. He don't act that nasty for nothing. What you think?"

"What was in the envelope?" I asked, not really wanting to deal with the whole subject.

"How I know?" Mary-Ann's voice got real high. "If I knew what was in the envelope, I wouldn't be asking nobody why it had his name on it. I'd know."

I told her I'd talk to her about it when I saw her, and she got mad and said that I didn't care about anything except myself. I let her talk until she got mad enough to hang up, and then I went over to Lenox Avenue and shot some pool.

I didn't have anything to do later, and so I went back over to the center, and Paul and Walter were there playing tonk. I wanted to talk to Paul about what Mary-Ann had said, but I didn't want to talk in front of Walter. I played tonk with them until I saw that I wasn't going to have any luck, and then I just watched them. I was thinking about going to a flick, but there wasn't anything I wanted to see in the neighborhood and I didn't have enough money to go downtown. I was torn between watching television and trying to borrow some money from Walter, who was winning at tonk, when somebody rapped on the door. Paul looked at me and opened the door. It was Cal.

> Your feets too big,
> I really hates you 'cause your feets too big . . .

I had tried to push Cal out of my mind after he hadn't shown up with the uniforms, and thought I had. Now, when I saw him, everything just jumped up in me, and I felt I couldn't control myself. He had a big box in his arms, and he put it down on the bench we used for a desk and started opening it. Maybe they were talking, I don't know.

I felt myself getting up and knew I was yelling at Cal, calling him names, asking him where the hell he had been. It was like seeing a movie. Walter and Paul turned and looked at me. Cal reaching slowly into the box and pulling out a uniform and handing it to me, then the uniform flying across the room. I reached in the back of the locker and got that old .32 pistol. Walter and Paul were yelling at me, and all the time Cal was standing there next to the uniforms. I was still screaming and half crying as Paul reached for the gun. He tried to push it down, and I tried to get it back up. I had both hands on it when it went off.

I thought I had shot my hand off. The pain went up my arm like somebody was running an iron up my veins. I fell back and squeezed my fingers together the best I could. I started to look at it but turned away when I saw the blood.

I heard myself screaming from the pain and cursing from the anger that was almost as bad as the pain. I fell to the floor, still holding my hand, and Paul and Walter were holding me. Cal got a bottle of whiskey and poured some of that on the place I had shot myself. It hurt as much as the shot did. I tried to fight my way up, but they held me down. I heard Cal tell Paul and Walter to leave. When they left, Cal took some bandages and tapes, stuff we used to tape our ankles when we played, and started bandaging my hand.

"It don't look so bad," he said. "You didn't get no bone. The way you was hollering I thought you had shot your finger off or something. No, all you got here is a lot of hurt."

He finished bandaging the hand and then sat down. Paul had been drinking a soda, and Cal sniffed it and then drank it. I was still breathing hard, like I had been running or something, and didn't say nothing until I had caught my breath good.

"I should have blown your butt away," I said.

"It's a wonder that piece of gun didn't blow your hand away."

"Where you been?"

"Looking around to see if I could find myself," Cal said.

"What bottle you look in?" I asked.

"Where we been don't matter so much as where we are now, do it?" He stood up and held up one of the uniforms. "And where I am right now is here with the uniforms and a place for us to practice starting tomorrow. You know where Lincoln Center is?"

I nodded.

"Well, you get the team there tomorrow morning at ten. I'll meet you at the fountain, and maybe we can get on with making a team. That okay by you? Or you going to get mad and shoot at yourself again?"

I wanted to say something else to him, but I couldn't. He put the uniform he had taken out back

into the box, fixed his shirt in his pants, and said he'd
see me in the morning.

When he left, I sat on the floor for a while and tried
to figure out what had went down. I hadn't thought
the cat's not showing up had bothered me so much,
but it had. I was glad that he was back, and I felt
funny about that, too.

Paul came back into the office. "Hey, man, you
okay? What happened to you, man?"

"Go to hell," I said.

3

We hit Lincoln Center with our bags and stuff and were looking around for Cal, and this white guy comes over and asks us were we the Alvin Ailey dancers.

"Yeah," Ox said, "but only now we ain't going to be dancing in no alleys anymore."

The guy looked at Ox like he was crazy or something and put on this frozen little smile and backed away. We sat around the pool, checking out the chicks and just digging everything and digging everybody digging us. Finally Cal shows, and he's wearing that jacket we bought for him. Breeze or Paul must have given it to him after he left the center. With our bags and that jacket everybody knew we were a team.

Walter Dean Myers

"Where we going, man? Paul asked.

"Back to school," Cal said.

We went over to Ninth Avenue and a school called Haaren. I had heard about Haaren, they had a pretty tough squad, but I had never been in the place. We went to the office, and Cal met the principal, a white dude. I don't know how he got to know all of these people, this principal, Sweet Man, or how he got the gym in the first place, but I was a little proud of him. I didn't want to say nothing to him about it, but Paul ran it down.

"Hey, Cal, how'd you get this gym?"

"Me and Matt Lee used to play ball together," Cal said. "He's the principal here now. Guess you don't know who your real friends are sometimes."

We went into the visitors' locker room, and Cal told us to change. The locker room was pretty nice, too. I dug some of the guys trying to act cool, and I could dig where they were coming from.

"Hey, coach, where do we put our valuables?" Breeze asked.

This guy, Matt Lee, got a strongbox and put it on the table and said that he'd lock it up until we had finished for the day. Breeze, who had already stripped and put his clothes in one of the lockers, took out his Afro pick and dropped it in the strongbox.

"You call that a valuable?" I asked him.

"When you're as pretty as I am, it is," he said.

We practiced every day that week. Except it wasn't practice. We didn't run any plays, we didn't work out any strategy, nothing. Just simple stuff like going after loose balls. Cal had us going after loose balls so

38

much that anytime a ball would fall to the ground five guys would want to jump on it. Then we practiced boxing out and rebounding until all the fun went out of even being in a gym. My hand was still sore, but it wasn't that bad. Cal said that I was lucky it hadn't got infected.

"Hey, Mr. Coach." Jo-Jo was laying on the floor in a pool of sweat trying to catch his breath. "I just figured out something. This ain't basketball, man; this is torture with dribbling thrown in to fool the public!"

"It won't be like this much longer," Cal said.

"I'm glad to hear that," Jo-Jo said. "Because I think this is killing me."

"It won't be like this much longer," Cal went on, "because we're going to have to work harder from now on."

Jo-Jo started rattling off something in Spanish. If I hadn't been so tired, it might have been funny.

A day later Ox had to do something so he was going to miss practice, and Breeze said he had to miss, too. So Cal called off practice for that day. That is, he called it off for everybody except me.

Everybody had dug how Cal had been on my case. I'd do something the same way that everybody else did it, but he would find something wrong with it. Sometimes he wouldn't find anything wrong with it; he would just tell me to do something else.

"When you get the step on the man anywhere from the key in," he said, "just lay it up. *Don't* jam!"

"Why not?" I asked. "That's the best way to make sure you got the deuce!"

"Yeah, and the only way your man is going to recover," he said. "Because you got to take that dip step to get up high enough to jam."

I didn't give him a lot of static because I knew he was trying, even if he was wrong in some of the things he was putting down. There's nobody going to recover fast enough to stop me from jamming once I get the step inside the key. I knew how fast I was if Cal didn't.

When Cal called the practice off for everybody except me, I figured he was just going to be on my case again, but I didn't mind, really. In fact, I even dug it a little. But when we got to the gym, he was wearing his sneakers and told me to take the ball out. He was going to play against me, and right away I sensed that we were going through a manhood thing.

I took the ball out and went for the hoop as straight up as I could because I didn't want to hear his mouth talking about how fancy I was trying to get. But he was all over me, pushing at me with his body and all. I figured okay, if he wanted to play manhood games with me, I could play them, too. He was always talking about playing the game to the bust, so that's the way I started to play it, to the bust.

The first time I played against Cal he beat me, but only because he was hustling and I was cooling out. This time we both went at it. That was when I found out the sucker could play. I mean, he could definitely hoop.

"Fifteen baskets win," he said.

"You ain't going to last that long," I said. "You're gonna have a heart attack and die, old man."

Hoops

At first the gym was quiet, just me and him, the sound of the ball against the floor and the squeaking of our sneakers. I blew the first shot, and he took the ball behind the line and popped a jumper from about sixteen feet. Okay. Then he went around me for a lay-up, but the next time he tried it I threw it away. All the time he was running down this rap.

"Don't lose contact. Keep your hand on me, so you know where I am, so you can *feel* me getting ready to move. . . . Don't pull up if you get the step. . . . Why you backing off? . . . Where are your guts?"

We kept playing, and we were just about even when some students came into the gym. Some teachers came in, too. Two white chicks and an older black dude. They sat down and started watching us. Then that friend of Cal's came in with some more teachers. They were sitting just off the court.

"Don't switch hands on the lay-up," Cal said.

I didn't want him talking that stuff in front of people, so I went baseline, spun, and switched hands just to show him I could do it. When I did it, he slapped the ball away, but I got it back before it went out of bounds. I came back the same way, only this time I didn't spin. I went straight up. I switched hands in the air and put the ball against the boards. It rolled around the rim and fell off.

We played for a while longer, and then I walked off the court. He had 11 to my 5, and I couldn't get my game together. He watched me walk off the court, and then he went over and started talking to that Matt Lee dude. They were shaking hands and grinning like he was somebody.

A bell rang and all the teachers had to split and he came back over to me.

"You ready for a few more drills?" he said.

"I don't need all these drills, man," I said. "Last game I played I was high scorer. The game before that I was high scorer and MVP. You can save the Mickey Mouse drills."

"That ain't good enough."

"Good enough for me," I said.

"Guess it don't take much to please you," he said. "Shoot!"

He half passed, half threw the ball at me. I looked him in the eye, and he looked back at me. I was really getting bugged with him and he knew it and he didn't care. I turned and threw a jumper. Nothing but net! He went over and got the ball and stood where I did when I made the shot. He threw a jumper, and I watched it float through the air. His shot wasn't as pretty as mine, but he had a way of making the ball look like it was floating through the air. My shot rammed into the basket while his just sort of settled in. He got the ball again and threw it back to me.

"How deep you plan on getting into the game?" he said.

"I'd like to know that myself."

"It's a tough business in those streets when you get past eighteen," he said. "You see things you were dreaming about start to curl up and die, and you want to curl up and die with them."

"I'm out there on the streets every day, man," I said. I threw a jumper from the corner, and it went in clean.

"You got to learn to use your talent," he said, "really use your talent, and you got to cover yourself."

"What's your cover, coach?"

"You are, Lonnie. You're my cover."

I really couldn't get next to that. I waited for him to go on, but instead, he grabbed the ball and started towards the hoop. He took off from the foul line, bringing the ball up from the dribble with one hand and hooking it in. It was a smooth move.

"That's pretty nice," I said.

"That was my shot when I was a kid," he said. "Used to drive suckers wild with that shot. I was playing in this big game one time when I came down the court and all of a sudden I was just doing it. I tried to figure out later where it had come from. And the only thing I could figure was that it was what I needed when I used it. I needed it, and it came."

He tried to show me the shot, how he controlled the ball from the dribble. His hands were bigger than mine, and half the time I tried it, the ball just went up in the air. But I could feel it. The way he explained the shot I could feel it. For the first time I felt that I had something that nobody else had. That maybe, just maybe, my game was a little deeper than a lot of other guys' games. It felt good.

Paul was never alone anymore. I went by the center, and he was there with one of his la-di-da friends. We didn't take people to the center unless they were okay. This cat had a big button on his jacket that said something about Justice for Native Americans. I didn't dig cats that wore signs on themselves.

"Hey, Paul, where you been?" I asked.

"Oh, I've been working with my friend, trying to get a book drive together," he said.

"Lenny," the cat said. "Lenny Travis."

He stuck out his hand, and I shook it. He had soft hands, and I wondered if he was funny or something. I didn't want to say nothing about his hands, so I asked him where he lived.

"Riverdale," he said. "Not far from the Russian embassy."

"Riverdale? Ain't that where the rich people live?"

He nodded.

"Lenny, this is Lonnie Jackson," Paul said.

"What's the button for?" I asked.

"It's in support of the American Indian," he said.

"What you doing for the Indians?" I asked.

"Well, for one thing," he said, looking around at Paul, "I'm wearing this button to advertise the fact that they aren't getting justice now."

"Why don't you do for your own?" I asked him. "Or don't you want to get involved with *us*?"

"What did you ever do for your own people?" Paul asked.

That got me mad because I felt I was being chumped off. I sat down in a chair and listened while Paul and Lenny talked about the book drive for the Native Americans. Then Paul started talking to Lenny about playing ball, and it was pretty clear that Paul had brought Lenny around to try out for the team. He looked too soft to be a ballplayer. But they were talking about how he played for some school, so I guess he must have had some kind of a game. I listened to their phony talk until I got tired of it.

Paul was talking just like Lenny, like he had a mouthful of cornflakes he didn't want to get any spit on.

"How long you going to be around, Paul?" I said. "I want to talk to you about something."

"We're waiting for my sister and her friend," Lenny said. "Her friend just came to the city from Boston about two weeks ago. Paul and I flew up and helped her pack her things and shipped them, and then we all flew down together."

I looked at Paul, and he looked away. He'd told me something about going to see his aunt a couple of weeks ago. He didn't say anything about flying to Boston. I told him I'd check him out later and started to leave. Just as I was going out of the door these two chicks came in.

One of them had to be Lenny's sister. She was thin and light-skinned like he was. The other one was light-skinned, too, almost white. It like to broke Paul's face to introduce me, but he did. Lenny's sister was named Joni, and the other chick was Leora.

The tournament, Cal explained, wasn't so much to see who won or lost but was a showcase for scouts all over the country. They were supposed to be coming to New York to look at ballplayers who hadn't been playing high school ball and who might have been overlooked because they weren't on a good team.

"But the thing is this," Cal said. "The first few games will be a round-robin practice round, and there won't be many scouts around. Then, after the round-robin part is done, you get into the elimination part. That's why they call it the Tournament of

Champions. There's all these divisions all over the city, and the champion of each division will get to play in the eliminations.

"Now check this out. Even though it's supposed to be a showcase, the idea of winning or losing is important. Everybody looks at a winner and says that he's good. And to be a winner in basketball, you have to have a team effort. If you didn't come to play ball, then you might as well not be here at all. Is that clear?"

Everybody said it was clear. The first game we were supposed to play was against the Morningside Comanches. I had seen them play a couple of times. They weren't much except for this guy they called Stealer John. Stealer John had a nice game. He was one of these guys that could stay high all the time and still keep his game together. He looked about forty-nine years old, but he was supposed to be the same age as me. I figured I'd be holding him.

Everything would have been cool except for Lenny. Cal put Lenny on the team and made Jo-Jo sit on the bench. Lenny's game was a gym game. He was the kind of cat that could play okay with about nine referees watching that nobody touched him, but he wasn't much in the playground. Cal said that he would help the team play together better.

When we got to the gym for the first game, there was a crowd there. I was surprised because mostly these tournament games didn't amount to much. There were a few white guys there in suits—I figured they must have been scouts or something.

Stealer John got the opening tap and drove right for the basket. He went up and jammed, and everybody on the sideline started calling out his name. It was like a chant. STEAL-LER! STEAL-LER! Paul brought the ball down and tried a behind-the-back pass to Ox, and Stealer intercepted the ball and started down-court again. He slowed the ball up when I got to it. Then he started moving to my right at the top of the key. He pointed to a spot on my right, and I thought that he was pointing to a spot for somebody to set a pick. I looked over, and he faked to my left. Then I jumped to the left and he went around me on the right side and I slipped and he jammed. That was his second jam in a row.

We went down, and Lenny fed me the ball, cutting across the lane. Stealer was on me, but I had half a step on him. I spotted Ox under the hoop, waving his arms. I could have either passed or went for the bucket myself. I went for the bucket. Ox's man, he must have lost Ox, so he switched over on me, came up, and threw my shot away. They scored again.

Paul hit a jumper. Then I stole the ball and got ahead of everybody and went up for the jam and hit the rim. The ball bounced out to Stealer, and he was off. I went after him, and when he put a move on to go around Lenny, I caught up with him. He started a drive, only he dribbled the ball too high and I went for it and got a piece of it and he went into me and we both fell down. They called a two-shot foul on me, and then there's Jo-Jo tapping me on the shoulder and telling me I'm out the game.

"What did you take me out for?" I asked Cal.

"You're turning your head on defense—"

"I didn't turn my head!"

"I saw you! That's why he got around you!"

47

"I was going for the steal! You said to look for the ball!"

Cal started sounding off at me. His shirt collar was open, and the veins in his neck stuck out. I sat down on the bench and watched as the Comanches ran up and down the court. It was a sloppy game, and they were winning easy. No matter what Stealer did they were yelling for him. Cal put Lenny on him, and he styled on Lenny like he wasn't even there. Even the referees were cracking on us. Ox was getting some respect around the boards, but Paul was so anxious to make Lenny look good he wasn't doing a thing. At half time they were up 74 to 54.

We went into the locker room and sat down. Cal didn't say anything. He just started getting his stuff together like he was going to leave. Everybody looked at him, but nobody said anything. Then Cal was standing in front of the mirror, picking out his hair, when Ox asked him what he wanted us to do in the second half.

"Do?" He turned around and looked at Ox. "What you asking me for? You playing your own game, ain't you? Everybody's playing for themselves, right? You ain't passing the ball. I know about playing basketball, I don't know what you're doing out there. Maybe you like the way they are laughing at you."

"You sitting Lonnie out don't help none," Jo-Jo said.

"Lonnie is sweet on Stealer John," Cal said. "You see the way he keeps giving him everything he wants. 'Go by me, Mr. John. Go on to the basket, Mr. Stealer. You want this rebound, Mr. John?' "

Hoops

"Well, look, Cal," I said. "You don't want me playing, I won't play!"

"That's right," Cal said. "Go on home. Because it takes a man to have enough pride to go out there and play the second half like he means it. And I don't think you guys are men enough!"

I walked out and went back into the gym. I wasn't sure what I was going to do or where I was going. I looked and Ox was with me and so was Jo-Jo. The others started out, too. I went down to the bench and sat on it.

"Where's your coach?" the referee asked.

"He's sick," somebody said.

"Well, let's get going."

I went out on the floor and looked for Stealer John. He wasn't on the court. I looked again. They were starting their scrubs!

Roy got the tap to Jo-Jo, who went all the way down the lane for the quick two. They came down and pulled a nice play with a couple of switches, but the cat that went for the hoop blew, and the rebound came out to Breeze. He brought it to the top of the key and then hit Paul with a bounce pass for another basket.

They went to inbound the ball and Jo-Jo jumped at the guy taking the ball out and the ball came in wild. I got it and hit a short jumper. Then their guy got jumpy and stepped into the court when he was taking the ball out, and the ref turned it over to us on the violation. We scored again, and they called time-out.

"Come on, we got to tighten up," Paul was saying.

49

Walter Dean Myers

I looked over to the scorer's table, and they were
bringing their first five back in. I looked over to our
bench, and I saw Cal standing behind some other
dudes. Okay, he wanted to know what we were made
of, he'd find out.

Stealer John brought the ball down, and I kept my
hand on him the whole time. He passed the ball off
but called for it right back. I was right on him. I
didn't let him breathe for a minute. Finally he backed
himself into a spot where Paul could double-team him.
I saw it and figured he'd move the ball away from
Paul and I'd have a chance for it. Paul came over,
and I saw his man start a cut towards the basket.
Maybe Stealer John would have passed the ball to
the cutting man or maybe he would have forced the
shot up, but he never got the chance. I had the ball
and started down the court. I couldn't hear anybody
after me, but I put the ball on the backboard anyway
for another deuce.

They called another time-out.

"You gonna pay for that, sucker!" Stealer John
pointed at me as he went to his bench. It made me feel
good that he was mad.

The rest of the game went down like death in an
old folks' home. Not a smile, not a moment everybody's mind wasn't in it. They were playing ball like
they were professionals or something. But we came
back slow but steady. People watching got real quiet,
and the game was being played by everybody just the
way it was supposed to be. When we got six points
away, the buzzer went off. We lost.

We got in the locker room, and I was so tired I

couldn't even sit down straight. Cal was handing out towels. He gave us some Gatorade and salt tablets, too.

A guy who had been hanging around the gym came in and started congratulating everybody.

"You got a nice team, coach," he said, handing Cal a card. "You got some real classy ballplayers. You don't mind if I tell them how good I thought they were?"

"I mind!" Cal looked at the guy like he had said something about Cal's mama or something. Then he threw the guy's card on the floor.

The guy shrugged and walked out.

Paul picked up the guy's card and looked at it and then handed it to Ox.

"Hey, coach." Ox was holding the guy's card. "That cat was a scout!"

"I don't want any of you guys talking to nobody without clearing it with me first!" Cal said.

"I don't know what you talking about, man," Ox said. "You said this tournament was about having coaches see us, didn't you?"

"Yeah, that's what it's all about," Cal said. There was sweat around his mouth, but the rest of his face was dry. "They all come on like Big Daddy, too. But just like every daddy, they got their own family to feed. He's going to tell you anything you want to hear as long as he can get you to play for his team. That's how he gets paid, by delivering the right flesh to the right team. Then, if they can't get what flesh they want, they get a whole lot of backups, just so they can justify their expense accounts.

"I've seen guys like you thinking that some big

school is interested in them because they've talked to a scout. You know for every guy that makes a team some scout has talked to twenty or thirty guys around the country and said the school was interested? You turn down five real chances for some fabulous school and go there to find you going up against a hundred guys just to make the junior varsity. Now can we talk about the game?"

"Yeah, go ahead, man." Paul was already getting into his street clothes.

"Let me ask you guys something." Cal was stuffing all the towels into a bag. "You guys win or lose out there today?"

"You know we lost, coach," Paul said.

"Did you have to lose?"

No one said anything.

"Who here thinks you lost because the other team was better than you were?"

No one said anything.

"Then let's all have two minutes of silence." Cal stood up and bowed his head. "We got young black men here who choose to lose instead of winning. That's something we should all have a moment of silence for. That's an opportunity we let die. Just give me two minutes of silence."

It was a long two minutes. At first it was uncomfortable, then it was embarrassing, and then I started to feel just a little ashamed of myself. After the two minutes were up, Cal told us how proud he was of how we had played the second half. It was too bad, he said, that we didn't think enough of ourselves to win when we had the choice.

By the time Joni and Leora got to the locker room,

we were all dressed and ready to go. We went down to the center and drank some sodas and a little wine that we had stashed there.

"What you guys celebrating?" Cal said.

I thought he was going to get into the thing about us losing again. Ox said he wasn't celebrating nothing, just having a few drinks.

"I'm just trying to relax after the game," Paul said.

"You go tell that to somebody who never played this game," Cal said. "You celebrating what you found out on that court this afternoon. You got yourselves a good team. You know it, the team that beat you know it, and everybody that saw the game knows it. You guys can play some ball, and that's what you're celebrating! Now somebody pass me a cool drink!"

When he said that, when he let it all out, we just tore loose. Because that's what we were thinking to ourselves. We were thinking that we played us some ball. I mean, we played us some B-A-L-L! We might have blown the game, but when we had our stuff together out on that court, it was together! Hearing Cal say it just put the icing on the cake.

"I think we could have beat the Knicks tonight," Paul said.

"Depends on whether or not Cartwright was hot," Cal said.

I took a look at that sucker, and he was really getting off on us having played so well. He was enjoying it as much as we were. He danced around with Joni and Leora until they split, and then one by one everybody left until it was just me and him left. We joked around until I was just about high, and then we locked up the center and split, too.

"Where you going, man?" Cal asked.

"I don't know," I said. "Maybe I'll follow you home. We can't be letting our coach out too late."

"Well, you are welcome to accompany me to my abode," he said. "And when you get there, you rest your load or use the commode, or you can just tip your hat and hit the road."

Cal and I walked toward his place. I wasn't sure when we started out if I was going to go in with him; I just wanted to drag out the day as long as I could. We rapped as we went uptown to where he lived, mostly about basketball and about the way the neighborhood had changed.

"Yeah," Cal said, "it's gone down a lot, you know. When the white folks found out they weren't welcome, they made sure they weren't going to leave anything up here that anybody would want. Close down the hospitals, close down the schools, they'd probably close down the streets if we'd let them."

"Yeah, it can be a ratty place to live," I said.

"On the other hand." Cal looked at me with a big grin. "Harlem ain't Paris, and Harlem ain't Rome. It may not suit you, but I call it home."

"Where you get all them corny sayings?" I asked. "The first time I saw you you were talking something about big feet. You probably don't even remember that now."

"Your feets too big . . ." He started singing that song again. "I really *hates* you 'cause your feets too big."

"That is one crazy song," I said. "I never heard that song before."

"Me and my woman, that was our song," he said.

"Here's where I live. That's an old Fats Waller song. I went up to see Aggie one day, and well, she was something special to me. I asked her if she could really go for a guy like me, something like that. She came over and sat next to me and started singing that song.

> Your feets too big.
> Don't want you 'cause your feets too big.

"That was the night we fell in love. Or at least the night we both knew it."

"What is it like being married?" I asked. He had gone in this apartment, and I waited until he had found the light switch and turned it on. It wasn't nothing to brag about, that was for sure.

"What's it like being married? Really married?" He looked at me. "I don't know. I always had one foot out the door and one foot in."

"Yeah, that's the way I am, too," I said. "I can't see getting next to a broad but one way, you dig?"

"You want another taste?" Cal asked. He was fumbling through a closet.

"Yeah, we ain't playing tomorrow."

"You sure played today," he said, "for a half anyway."

"You really dig this tournament thing, huh? I mean, what are you getting out of it?"

"Told you," he said. He held two glasses up to the light to see if they were clean. He wiped one on his shirt and then held them both up again. "You're my cover. You get the dirty glass, too."

"Cover for what?" I asked.

"Don't worry about it."

"You just want to play mysterious, that's all," I said. "Talking about me being your cover . . . acting all funny when that Casey dude came in the locker room."

"That *Casey* dude?" Cal stopped pouring the whiskey and looked at me. "How do you know his name is Casey?"

"I saw him before," I said. "He said some of the kids at Haaren who had seen you and me playing told him about me."

"What else he say?"

"You going to pour that drink or what?"

"I asked you what else did he say, and what did he offer you?" Cal's voice got cold, and he looked at me as if I had said something wrong. I started to shrug it off, but he just stared at me.

"He said that maybe he could get me into a college," I said. "Or something like that. Anyway, I figured I'd try out for one of the eastern leagues. He said that if I wasn't interested in college, maybe he could help me work something out."

"What did he offer you, and did you take it?"

"He gave me his card and a twenty-dollar bill. He said it was money to make the call with," I said. "Say, look, what are you getting so uptight for? The dude laid twenty dollars on me. I didn't kill nobody. I didn't steal nothing from nobody. He just gave me the money for nothing."

"When's the last time somebody gave you something for nothing?"

"Man, cut this lame stuff," I said. I was really tired

of it. "Who made you the white knight all of a sudden?"

"Hey, maybe I am the white knight, or maybe I'm Little Red Riding Hood or somebody," he said, putting the glasses down. "How's that: Cal Jones, also known as Little Red Riding Hood?"

"If you getting this way from that stuff you drinking, you don't have to pour me none," I said. "In fact, it's getting kinda late, so maybe I just better get going."

"No, wait a minute," he said. He got down on his knees in front of an old trunk and dug in a pile of clothes until he came to one of those books that people keep their family pictures in. He handed it to me.

"It's a scrapbook."

"Yeah. I'm going to let you look at it, Lonnie," he said. "I don't want you to say nothing to nobody about it, you understand?"

"I ain't mouthy," I said. "You don't want nobody to know about your scrapbook, ain't nobody going to know."

"You're right about one thing," he said. "It is scrap. That's my life you got there in your hands. Scraps. Pieces of things stuck in an old book that nobody knows about."

I opened the book, and it was like one of those old black-and-white movies you see on television sometime. The pictures were almost all cut from newspapers, and were turning yellow. They were all about basketball games.

"This you?" I asked. "Spider Jones?"

"Used to be . . . what game you on now?"

"DeWitt Clinton."

"I scored fifty points that game—"

"Says here forty-eight!"

I went on and saw that he had played for City College. The more I read, the better he was getting. The first few pages were about high school games, and maybe there would be a paragraph or two or just a few lines. Then there were tournaments and college games. They had pictures of him holding a Most Valuable Player award over his head. He looked different then, skinny, with long arms and legs. I could see why they called him Spider.

The magazine pieces were the best. They had him on an All-American team. He was in color, too. The picture made him look darker than he was, but you could still tell it was him if you looked close.

"I ain't taking nothing from you, man, but how come you didn't turn pro?" I asked.

"Mostly because you didn't turn enough pages," he said.

I turned a few more pages. There were pictures of him playing in the NIT and the Rucker Tournament. And then there was a headline that said: "Big O burns rookie!" There he was, holding Oscar Robertson! I didn't believe it! Cal had played pro ball. I couldn't read fast enough. He had played with the best in the world. I kept looking up at him to see if it was the same guy.

"You played pro!"

"I played pro!"

"What happened?"

"You heard about Davey Blue?" He reached over

and got the bottle again. "Same thing happened to me."

He turned a couple of pages and pointed to a small article. He had underlined some words: "associating with known gamblers and behaving in a manner detrimental to the interests of the National Basketball Association . . ."

"You do it?"

"Yeah, I did it."

"Man . . ." I couldn't think of anything to say. "At least Blue was innocent."

"Dave Blue was used, and I was used," he said. "The only difference was that he didn't know he was being used because he didn't see it. I didn't know I was being used because I didn't want to see it."

"White cats do it to you?"

"Ain't nobody did anything to me," he said. "I did it to myself. A man come up to me with a fistful of money, and I took it. Nobody gives you something for nothing, and I knew it."

"What did you do, throw a game?"

"I was what they called a shaver. The gamblers figure out how much a team should win by. They figure you should win by five points, maybe seven. Then that's the spread. Somebody want to bet some money on you they got to give up the points in the spread. If we were supposed to win by five, I'd see to it that we only won by three or four. If we were supposed to win by three or four, I'd try to cut it down to a deuce."

"That don't sound so bad, man; you was still winning."

"Walking down the street naked don't sound too

bad either until they put your behind in jail. . . . I knew what I was doing. It wasn't about the money either. I was making more money than I ever had. I was on top of the world, looking down from a silver cloud. The money the guy gave me was chump change. But he told me I was being slick, and I listened to him. The only thing I ever had in life was my game, Lonnie. It was so sweet, people who didn't know a thing about it would come to see me play. You know how women come to the games sometimes. They want to see your body in the air doing things that other cats can't do. You know how that feels to you when you're doing it. I would touch the ball and I would know something was going to happen. . . . It was a kind of magic. It made me something that a million other guys would pay to watch.

"That's what I sold for the chump change. I sold my *game*! It got so that I hated to play. I'd go out there and warm up with the other guys, and all I could think about was what I was going to do. I still had a game, but there would come times when I had to pull it together, when I had to play it to the bust to keep from losing, and I just couldn't do it.

"I told the cat that gave me the bread that I couldn't do it anymore, and he looked at me and he just laughed. We were sitting in the lobby of the Shoreham Hotel in Washington. He looked at me when I said I wouldn't shave any more points for him, and then he ordered a bottle of liquor and acted like he had never heard what I said. I had already sold my game.

"You know what you love in this life? You love

what makes you stand the tallest. It can be your woman, your country, your job. I loved basketball, Lonnie. It was what I had. I had it, and I threw it away. Hey, can you dig it? The one thing that I had, the one gift, and I threw it away, can you dig it?"

Cal was really upset. His whole body was shaking. I stood up and started to put my hand on him, and then I walked away. I didn't want to see him like that, but I didn't know what to do. There was a record player on the bureau and a record on it. I turned it on and put the arm on the record as it started to spin. It was a chick singing.

Give me red lipstick . . .
And a shot of good booze

It was a slow blues. I listened to it as Cal got himself together. I didn't think about anything, mostly because I didn't know what to think about. I sat down in an old rocking chair he had and put my feet on the table.

4

I was sitting on the stoop in front of the Grant when Paul comes by with Lenny and Joni. Far as I'm concerned, Lenny still looks like a faggot.

"Hey, Lonnie, how's it going?" Lenny talks like he's afraid his teeth are going to break or something.

"Okay," I said. "Where you people headed?"

"Paul's just showing us around the neighborhood," Lenny says. "This place is something else!"

"You ought to get yourself one of them buses that be bringing white folks through," I said, "if you want to see the real ghett-o!"

Paul started looking around like he was embarrassed

to even be there. Then he started talking some jive about when the next practice was going to be. He knew when it was going to be the same as me. I didn't even answer him, but Lenny did.

"We're going out to the Nassau Coliseum later on to see The Spinners and Tyrone Davis. You want to come?"

"How much are the tickets?"

"Paul got them," Joni said, squeezing his arm. "How much were they, Paul?"

"Fifteen dollars," he said, half under his breath.

"I ain't going," I said.

They hemmed and hawed for a while longer, and then Lenny said that they had to be going. Fifteen dollars times three was forty-five dollars. I couldn't figure out how Paul got that kind of bread. I knew he wasn't working, and I knew his moms wasn't coming up with no bread like that to send him to the Coliseum. Then I remembered what Mary-Ann had been saying about Paul's name being on an envelope in Tyrone's office at the club she works in. I couldn't make it add up.

I started thinking more about Cal playing pro ball, and the truth was that I wanted to tell somebody. Not that I wanted somebody to know about it so bad, but I just wanted to talk about it to somebody so I could get it straight in my own mind. Then I had a thought that really knocked me out. I would take Mary-Ann over to see Cal, and then maybe I would tell her, if she liked him.

I went over to Paul's place and knocked on the door, and Freddie, Paul's brother, opened it. Soon as he saw it was me he got into his Muhammad Ali stance and went into a little jive shuffle. I dug it. Freddie was a nice kid. I told him there was a roach near his foot and he looked down and I gave him a little uppercut. That ticked him off because he was always falling for something like that.

"Mary-Ann home?"

"Yeah," he said—he was still pouting—"but she's sleeping."

"Your mama home?"

"No, just me and Mary-Ann," he said, "and I wouldn't be here if I had a quarter!"

I gave him a quarter, and he split. Mary-Ann usually slept over at Tyrone's place. When she did sleep at home, it would be when Paul wasn't home and she'd sleep in his bed. I went into Paul's room, and she was laying there with the covers up around her head.

I got on the bed and started blowing in her ear.

First she pulled the cover up around her ear, but I just pulled it away and started blowing in her ear again. Then she started murmuring something in her sleep. I did that for another minute or so, and it still didn't seem that she was going to wake up, so finally I shook her by the shoulder. If she didn't move around in her sleep, I would have thought she was dead because she didn't wake up until I just about shook her head off.

"What you doing here?" she asked. Her eyes were only half opened, and she had her head tilted back so she could see through the slits.

"I got an idea," I said.

"What kind of idea?"

"I want you to meet Cal."

"Who's Cal?" she asked. "Ain't he that wino you were talking about?"

"He's okay," I said. "I really dig the guy, and I want you to meet him."

"Why?" She opened her eyes full for the first time and looked at me.

"You know you got some pretty eyes, girl," I said.

"Yeah? What else?"

"You mean about Cal?"

"No, I mean about my pretty eyes," she said. Then she pulled the sheet down her arm. "How about this dynamite shoulder?"

"Come on, be serious," I said.

"When we going to meet him?" she asked. She slipped out of bed, and she had on a brown slip with lace on the bottom that lay against her thigh and sent goose pimples up my back. She stretched and then grabbed a blouse from the drawer as I tried to drag my mind back to what I had been thinking about.

"He's probably over at the center now," I said. "We could go over there and you can meet him."

"You still didn't tell me why you want me to meet him," she said.

"I just do," I said, "that's all."

"Do I have to meet your mother, too?" she asked. She was sitting on the edge of the bed, putting on some little half socks.

"What's that supposed to mean?" I asked. "You've met my mother a lot of times."

"Well, usually, when a guy starts bringing his girl to meet his parents and stuff . . ."

"He ain't my father, he's just the . . . what you want

to go and say something like that for?" I asked. "You starting some dozens with me?"

"Hey, man, cool out," she said. "I didn't mean nothing. What you getting all upset about? I was just kidding in the first place!"

"Well, I don't dig that kind of kidding," I said, knowing I was madder than I should have been. "Forget the whole thing, I'm going."

"Lonnie Jackson, will you get out of yourself for a minute?"

"Yeah." I sat down.

"Why are you so hard to get next to?" she asked. "You're about as fine as you want to be until you find yourself getting close to somebody."

"How you know that, girl?" I asked.

"How you know that, *girl*?" She mimicked me. "You say 'girl' like girl is something bad when I start getting close to you. You think because you acting like some kind of wild animal, I can't deal with you? You can't get me off your trail that easy. I'll come after you just like a big-game hunter. I'm going to track you down, stay on your trail until I get you in a corner, and then I'm going to be there when you come out scratching and clawing. And I'm going to be scratching and clawing, too. It's going to be good. Mary-Ann, the big-game hunter. How's that sound?"

"You sound dangerous."

"I am, sugar, you might as well get that straight from the get-go!"

I kissed her and, just a little, not a lot . . . just a little . . . I was scared of her. Maybe she was as dangerous as she said she was.

* * *

On the way over to the center I told her about Paul and Lenny going over to the Nassau Coliseum. She said that Paul had a lot of money recently and she didn't know where he was getting it from. When she asked him, he told her to mind her business.

"He's always telling me that," Mary-Ann said. "But usually he acts like it's no big thing. When I asked him the other day, he started going through a lot of changes."

"He's trying to keep up with those la-di-das from uptown," I said. "When they get tired of him, they'll shake him loose and won't even remember his name."

We got over to the center, and Ox was in talking to Cal. He had Sparrow on his shoulder. We talked around for a while, and then I gave Ox the sign to split.

"Say, coach." I closed the door behind Ox and hoped that nobody else would come in. "I want you to meet Mary-Ann."

"Hey, hello." Cal nodded towards her.

"I've heard a lot about you," Mary-Ann said.

"Oh, that's nice," Cal said.

He didn't say anything else, and I didn't say anything. We just sat there for a minute.

"This is a nice little place you have here," Mary-Ann said.

"What, er . . . what can I do for you?" Cal asked.

"Like what?" I asked.

"Well . . ." He looked over at Mary-Ann. "Is Mary-Ann your lady?"

"Yeah, I guess so," I said.

"Man, well, why didn't you say something?" Cal stood up and came around the desk and shook

Mary-Ann's hand. "Now I'm really glad to make your acquaintance, young lady. I didn't know why he brought you here. I thought she might be a backup guard or something."

Cal broke out some sodas, and we sat around and rapped for a while, and they hit it off real nice. It made me feel good, and when I took Mary-Ann back over to her mother's place, she was really happy.

"Look, I want to tell you something about Cal," I said. "But you got to keep it between you and me, dig?"

"Go ahead."

"He used to play pro ball," I said.

"Uh-huh."

"Uh-huh?" I looked at her. "I tell you the guy used to play pro ball and all you can say is uh-huh? He played with the Big O, he played with cats like Twyman and Baylor. This dude was so bad they wrote him up in all the papers and stuff."

"Hey, that's really good!" she said.

"You don't even know what I'm talking about, do you?"

"I know all the words, Lonnie," she said. "But I don't know how they feel coming out of you, dig? I mean, I just don't have anything that makes me feel that way. You got your heart set on playing pro ball, and I'm still waiting to set mine on something."

"Yeah. You know Cal could give me . . . not give me, not even teach me . . . what am I trying to say?"

"Help you."

"Yeah, that's right. He could help me with my game and everything."

"You gonna let him?"

"Am I gonna do what? Sure, that's what it's all about," I said. "He thinks I can make it, too."

"I'm surprised."

"Surprised? You seen me play, woman. You don't have to know that much about the game to know I can play."

"Not about your game, Lonnie All-Star. About you letting somebody help you."

"I don't need that much help," I said. "He's just showing me a few things, that's all."

"Things like what?" she asked.

"Like . . . I don't know, just things," I said. "Don't make a big deal over it."

Mary-Ann was right about me not letting a whole lot of people help me. I didn't let people help me because I didn't need it mostly. Besides that, it was just like Cal said, nobody gives you something for nothing. They'd either have something they'd want you to do for them or they'd want you to hang around them and act like you're grateful. I didn't know if Cal was going to turn out that way or not, but I really wanted to check him out. The cat really wasn't into that much, but I was really digging him. Yeah, he seemed okay, but I was still checking him out.

The next day after practice Cal asked me if I wanted to meet his old lady. I didn't want to, particularly, but I didn't have anything else to do, so I went.

The A train rocked back and forth as we headed uptown. There weren't too many people on it. At the far end of the car there were two teachers with their classes. The only thing was that the teachers were really young. I winked at one of them, and instead of turning away, she gave me a nice smile.

"I told you about Aggie?"

"You mentioned her," I said.

"When I first met her, she was singing," he said. "She's good, but she just couldn't get over."

"If she was that good, she should have made it," I said.

"Hey, man, you don't know nothing, do you?" He looked at me and shook his head. "Just because you good at something don't mean you *have* to make it. Especially us. Every time you see a black person who's got it halfway made you can bet there's a dozen more just as good as he is waiting for a chance. There's a lot of singers out here who can smoke anything you see on television. How many ugly singers you see making records and singing on television?"

"None, really," I said.

"Right. You think ugly people can't sing? They out there, but they can't make it. And for every black basketball player in the NBA under six ten, there's two more out here just as good who won't see the inside of the Garden unless he's got a ticket or a broom. Anybody that looks at a black guy and tells him that he can make it in basketball just because he's good is either lying or dumb. You got to be so special your feet don't touch the ground when you walk. People used to laugh when Satchel Paige used to say, 'Don't look back, something might be gaining on you.' Any black cat in the world that knows anything knows what old Satch meant.

"I remember one time a black football player came over to me in a hotel and told me how hard it was to make it in the National Football League. He said, the only thing that made it for him was that he could sew buttons on uniforms."

"Sew buttons on uniforms?"

"That's the same thing I said when he told me. He said he went to the tryouts thinking he was bad. He started telling them about his college record and how many yards he had gained. He said this red-neck coach looked at him and pointed to a ten-foot brick wall. The coach said, 'Boy, we got fifteen niggers in camp who can jump over that wall, we got ten that can run through it, and we got six that can run through it without messing up our uniforms, and we only got room on the squad for three. Now what can you do?'

"I knew a cat called Goat that had more moves than Ex-Lax. I knew another guy that used to come down to the park. We used to have those square metal backboards. He could jump up and put a quarter on the top of a backboard, then jump up and change the quarter for two dimes and a nickel. He could shoot, pass, and play defense. When they used to bring the white boys into Harlem to play in the Rucker Tournament, they wouldn't even let these cats play."

"If they were so good, how come they didn't play in the NBA?" I asked.

"One cat couldn't make it because he had a record; one cat was into dope; one couldn't make it because someone said that he *might* have done something.

They didn't like the way one cat looked, he had about three teeth missing. Any old thing. They got a thousand cats like us that can play this game, Lonnie. A thousand guys that have a game and looking for something to do with it."

We reached an apartment building on Manhattan Avenue, and Cal checked out his clothes in the mirror in the hallway. It was an old building, but it looked all right. Some of the tin was coming off the stairs and there were a few things written on the walls, but nothing too bad. I could tell that Cal was nervous.

"Hey, man." I was behind him walking up the stairs. "She do know we're coming, don't she?"

"Yeah," he said. "She knows I told her we're coming. But once I told her I was coming by, and it was a pretty important time, and I didn't show. So when I tell her now, she just takes it light, you know."

We got to the top floor and went to one of the apartments and rang the bell. There wasn't an answer, and Cal rang again. Still no answer. He knocked. Just when I figured there wasn't going to be no answer, the door opened.

I've always figured that if you want to know a guy, you got to check him out with his woman. Some guys are okay until they get around their woman; then they start thinking they're Superman or something. You can't say this to them and you can't say that to them because they think you're chumping them off in front of their woman. The first time I met Cal was when he was laying in the playground, so I knew he wasn't no bank teller or nothing like that. He had played ball and had paid some dues and stuff, too. So I figured I knew him. He was a pretty tough guy and wouldn't take too much off nobody. Then I seen him with Aggie.

He had bought a bottle of wine, the kind you got to open with a corkscrew. Well, she gives him a little peck on the cheek and goes on fixing some supper and talking light talk, and he's holding the bottle in his hand like he forgot it was even there.

"How come you holding the bottle in your hand?" I asked.

"Hmm?" He looked at me and then smiled this big smile and put the bottle on the table.

"So you play ball, too?" Aggie wiped her hands on the dishrag and turned towards me.

"A little," I said.

"He any good?" She turned to Cal.

"Yeah, he's nice, real nice," Cal said.

"He must be to get you back in the game," she said.

"Guess who I had a long conversation with this morning?" Cal said, undoing the bottle.

"Who?"

"Sweet Man Johnson."

"He still the same?"

"Yeah, he still the same," Cal said. "He ain't gonna never change."

"He's the only one," Aggie said. She went through a drawer full of junk and found a corkscrew and handed it to Cal. "Most of these people get more than two cents in the pocket, get their heads so big they can't get their hats on. I saw Richie the other day, you remember that guy everybody used to call Buddha?"

"Yeah," Cal said. "This cat was a Muslim when we first met him, see? Then a little bit later he turned to being Jewish. Then the last time we saw him he had joined the Jews for Jesus movement."

"Right." Aggie was stirring a frying pan full of onions and green peppers and sprinkling it with red pepper. "Anyway, I saw that fool the other day. He was on the downtown side of the A train platform, and I was on the uptown side, going to the hairdresser. He's yelling and everything, and then he comes busting over. Now, dig it, he runs up one flight of stairs, across the station, and down the other flight of stairs, just to give me this card that says 'Richard Thompson, Business Representative.' He missed his train trying to impress me. And guess what he's a business representative of? Avon Products!"

Me and Cal both laughed at that, but I was getting to feel really left out. It wasn't like they weren't talking to me, because they were. But I got the feeling I was supposed to leave, only I didn't know exactly how to pull it off. And maybe that wasn't it either. The thing was, like I said before, you got to see a guy with his woman before you really got to know him. With Aggie, Cal was different. He talked smoother, and they just seemed to touch bases in different places that I didn't know because I hadn't been there. "Remember this?" or "remember that?"

And Aggie was different, too. She had something, and I couldn't figure out what it was. She was nice-looking, real nice, but she wasn't sexy. Only she *was* sexy, but she wasn't the kind of sexy that you would say anything to her on the street. She was like Joni, Lenny's sister, in the way she carried herself. But she didn't talk any different than me or Cal. I was sitting there all through dinner trying to figure out how she was different. I knew she was different, though, and I could really see her getting next to a guy.

"So what else you been doing with yourself?" Cal asked.

"Oh, nothing," Aggie said. She and Cal were drinking coffee, and I was drinking the wine—it wasn't sweet enough, but it was what we had. "I went up and saw Nina Simone at City College the other day."

"You still go to those concerts."

"I hadn't been," she said, "but this guy wanted to go."

"Oh." I could see that when she mentioned another guy, it took something out of Cal. He looked away for a minute, and a kind of sadness came over his face. So quickly, though, that I wasn't sure that it wasn't just a shadow.

"I've been trying to do some writing, too," Aggie said. "My poetry isn't all that's it's cracked up to be, but if I get the music put to it, it'll be okay."

"You know, I wrote some—" It came out before I even realized it was going to.

"You write poetry?" Aggie looked at me and waited for an answer.

"No," I said, sorry I had opened my mouth about the story I had wrote. "It's just this little jive story. You know."

"What's it about?" Aggie stood up and took some paper out of the closet.

"Nothing much," I said.

"If you wrote it, then I would like to hear about it," Aggie said.

"I didn't know you wrote," Cal said.

"I was telling a story to Paul's little brother," I said.

They were both looking at me. "It sounded okay, so I wrote it down for some reason."

"What's it about?" Aggie asked. She was dead serious, too, like it was normal that I would go around writing stories.

"It's about a giraffe named Gordon," I said, looking right at Cal. "He's tall, dig, and he eats the leaves from the tops of trees. And everybody digs him because he's tall, but he gets tired of people saying how cool it is to be tall because he gets kind of . . . you know . . . ain't nobody else as tall as he is."

"I'd like to see it sometime," Aggie said. She said it like she really meant it.

"What did you write?" I asked Aggie.

"I don't have the tune finished yet," she said, "but it goes something like this:

> Honey, yes, I know it's love
> When I wake up in the mor-ning
> And you're the only thing
> That's on my miiind.
>
> And baby, yes, I know it's love
> When I'm looking for a reason
> And you're the only one
> That I can fiiind.
>
> Oh, sugar, yes, I know it's love
> When the summer sun comes burning,
> And it doesn't touch the warmth
> I feel for you.

Aggie could sing. Aggie could sing a bird right off a tree. The words she was singing were together, and so was the tune, but you didn't even have to listen to the words or the tune because she was singing all in between the words and the meaning didn't make as much sense as the feeling did. When she opened her mouth to sing, it was like she was a different person altogether. I felt like running outside and playing some ball for her, or doing something. I just wasn't used to people being that heavy. When she finished, Cal turned to me, and I could see his eyes getting red and I thought he was going to let go, but he got himself together.

"What do you think?" Aggie looked at me and then at Cal.

Later, when we were leaving, Aggie said that she was going down to buy a container of milk. I said I'd go, figuring that I'd give them a chance to be alone. Maybe I wouldn't even get the milk, I'd just go on to the Grant. But she said no, and she put on a sweater and we went downstairs.

"You can really do it," Cal said to Aggie. They were holding hands.

"You're just getting old," she said. "Anything sounds good to an old man."

"Who's getting old?" Cal sucked his stomach in. "You must be out of your mind, girl."

"You're getting old," she said. "I can see that hair getting kind of thin up there in front. You got to let me grease your hair sometimes."

"I ain't getting old," Cal said. "I'm faster than this turkey here."

"You can't even beat *me*," she said.

"See that lamppost down there," Cal said. "I'll give

you a head start and beat you so bad you'll think I'm sixteen years old."

"You think so?" Aggie said.

"I know so."

"Tie your shoes and I'll consider it."

When Cal looked down at his shoe, Aggie took off for the lamppost.

"Here I come! Here I come!" Cal shouted out.

When he shouted that, Aggie really started running. Cal didn't run at all; he just watched her. When she got to the lamppost, she turned and saw that he hadn't run. She watched him laughing as she leaned against the post, trying to catch her breath. And then, just as we got to where she was standing, her smiles changed to tears. She grabbed his shirt at the shoulders and held them and looked at him as if she was thinking of a way to throw him down or something. Then she kissed him.

"Take care of yourself, baby," she said. "Don't get yourself hurt."

Then she was gone. Even from where we stood, we could see she was still crying as she went.

I saw Mary-Ann in front of the State Office Building. At first I almost didn't recognize her. She looked different.

"Hey, what's happening?" I said. I started to lean over and kiss her on the cheek.

"Go to hell!" she said.

She started walking away, just like that, and I let her. I figured she'd see I wasn't chasing after her and stop, but she didn't. Finally I did go after her. I spoke to her again, but this time she didn't even answer. That's the way we walked all the way uptown. Only she was really hoofing. I had to walk fast to keep up with her. I figured that maybe she'd cool down by the time she got uptown, so I waited before I said anything else to her. But I did check her out, and I saw why she looked so different. The left side of her face was bruised and swollen. You could tell even though she was wearing shades.

"What happened to your face?" I asked. She had stopped near the park and sat on the end of one of the benches. I sat down next to her. She didn't answer me, and I just lay back against the bench and gave her all the time she needed. Finally she spoke.

"Paul slapped me," she said.

"Paul?"

"Yeah. First Tyrone called me a name, and then Paul slapped me," she said. "I got some more time, why don't you cut me or something?"

"You know I ain't that way."

"I *thought* Paul wasn't that way either," Mary-Ann said. She had calmed down a little, and now she was beginning to cry. The physical part of the hurting was over, and now the other part was taking over.

"What happened?"

"I was in the club talking to Jackie and Ebony, Tyrone's little daughter," Mary-Ann said. "Me and Jackie was just playing with her, saying things like when she was going to get married, that kind of thing. Tyrone's door is open, and he's calling somebody on the phone. Then he gets into an argument over the phone, which is no big thing for him. First he's asking whoever it was he was talking to about having lunch. They must have said no because he was like really coming on like he wanted to see them or something. So I figured it must be some white chick because that's what he digs most.

"Anyway, then he gets mad because the chick says she don't want to have lunch with him, I guess. He starts hollering over the phone, and then he slams it down. Me and Jackie don't pay him no mind. Even little Ebony don't pay him no mind. Then he sees me, and he tells me to go get my brother."

"What he want Paul for?"

"That's what I wanted to know," Mary-Ann said. "So I asked him, and that's when he sounded on me. Then I went home and told Paul what had happened, and he gets up to rush out to see what Tyrone wants. He don't say nothing about Tyrone sounding on me. I catch him by the arm as he's busting out the door, and he turns and slaps me! Now can you beat that?"

"Not really," I said.

"Well, if you could, I got another one for you," Mary-Ann went on. "I laid down for a while, then I went down and sat on the steps, feeling like change for about two cents when Nita comes up—"

"That Spanish chick?"

"Yeah, she come up and tells me that everybody is talking about how Paul done beat up some chick crosstown."

"Said *what*?"

"That's right." Mary-Ann's eyes were full of tears. "I'm going into Tyrone's drawer and get that envelope with Paul's name on it. That's got to have something to do with this mess."

I figured her to be right, but I didn't think she should take Tyrone too lightly. I asked her when she was going to do it, and she got up and said she was going to do it right then.

"I don't think that's too cool."

"Well, what else can I do?" Mary-Ann looked up at me. Either she was getting better-looking or I was looking at her different.

"You know when he's going to be away from the office?" I asked.

"He's supposed to be in Chicago for some big meeting tomorrow morning," Mary-Ann said. "He's leaving tonight."

We waited around until two thirty in the morning before going to the club. I had my piece, only I didn't let Mary-Ann know. If Tyrone did double back I wanted some heat to defend myself.

It was dark in Tyrone's office. I couldn't see my hand in front of my eyes. Mary-Ann had some matches, and we lit them and looked around the best we could, but they didn't help too much. Then I took my jacket off and put it on the floor in front of the door so you couldn't see the light coming from under the door, and we put on one of the lamps in Tyrone's office. We covered it with a cloth, so it gave some light but not too much. The desk drawers were locked, and none of the keys laying on the desk worked. I tried to pull them open, but that didn't work, and we figured it would take too long to try to pick the locks. Mary-Ann slipped out and went to her room and got the screwdriver that she used to change the television channels with. I jimmied open the middle drawer, and the rest came open. We looked for the envelope with Paul's name on it, and we found it along with some other envelopes and a list of names and numbers. Paul's name was on the list. Cal's name was on it, too. There was some cash in a box in the same drawer, and we took that and a few other things, including some stamps and a calculator, to make it look like a robbery. I got my coat and went over to the Grant, and Mary-Ann followed a few minutes later. I had the envelopes, and we went over them.

Two of them had IOUs in them, one from a cop that used to hang around the place, and one from somebody else. Then there was a list of names with numbers next to them which I figured was also money that Tyrone had lent people. I couldn't tell what some of the others were, and neither could Mary-Ann. We had saved the envelope with Paul's name on for last. I opened it up. They were checks. They were all welfare checks made out to people from around the block. Then I looked on the back of them and saw they had all been cashed at one place.

"How come he's got these checks in an envelope with Paul's name on it?" I said aloud to myself.

Mary-Ann took the checks from me again and looked at them.

"You see this check?" She showed me one of them that was made out to Mrs. Susan Jenkins.

"Yeah?"

"This check was stolen from the mailbox," Mary-Ann said. "I remember it was raining on the Friday after check day, and she said she had to go downtown and see about getting an emergency digit because her check and some others had been stolen."

Some of the checks were from the same date as that

one, and others were from different dates. They were all signed with the name on the front of the check, but you could tell they were all signed by the same person. I looked at the name of the store that was stamped on the back. It was over near Highbridge.

We counted the money we had taken—$160. Mary-Ann told me to keep it. We took everything else and put it in a bag and threw it down the garbage chute. We talked for a while, and I tried to get next to Mary-Ann, but she said she wanted to go back over to the club to sleep, just so everything would look normal. I told her she could go over later, but she still wasn't in the mood.

"You going to check out that store tomorrow?" she asked.

"Yeah," I said.

On my way to the Grant I felt every eye on the street was on my back. It wasn't a good feeling.

5

When I got up, it was nearly eleven o'clock. I remembered I was supposed to go over to my moms's pad. I got dressed and went downstairs.

"It's about time you got your butt up," Harrison said. "I called you nearly an hour ago!"

"You called *me*?"

"Yeah, I shook your shoulder, too," he said.

"What I say?"

He made a funny noise like a guy that didn't want to wake up, and I figured it sounded like me. It sounded pretty funny, too. Only when he saw me smile, he started running it into the ground. I asked him what he was trying to wake me up for, and he said my mother was wondering where I was.

I went over to her house and listened to her mouth about how she could be laying up there with a heart attack and die before I came to see her.

"The rats be done eat me up before you come to see me!" she said. "Don't you come crying when they lay this old gray head down beneath the ground, boy. You hear that?"

"Yeah, I hear that."

"When I'm dead and gone, you go on and ignore me just like you doing now," she said, "because as God is my secret judge, I can't stand to see nobody crying and carrying on at no funeral when they didn't give two cents for the body when it had life in it."

"Yes, ma'am."

"But soon it *will* be done . . ." she went on.

I knew the rest of the sermon by heart. *Trouble of this world.*

"Trouble of this world . . ."

One more time.

"Trouble of this world . . . Yes, Jesus . . ."

The sermon went on a little longer than it usually did and I opened the refrigerator and saw that mama had picked up a little taste. I poured myself some of the rum, drowned that bad boy in some Coke, and drank it. Then I asked her if she had finished shopping, and she went into how she had to give some other mother's son fifty cents to carry the package up the stairs that her son should have carried. Amen.

I looked in the refrigerator, and it was jammed full

of food. I was glad I hadn't been around to carry that load.

I kissed her and split.

I went over to Highbridge and went into the store that cashed the checks. It was in an arcade. I looked through some of the magazines, which were supposed to be for sale but were months old. The whole time these junkies kept coming in and heading for the back, and I knew they were back there shooting up on whatever they were on. The cat that ran the place was named Ugly. That was what his daddy named him when he was born. They got the name wrong because they should have named him Ugly Damn Dog, because that's what he was. He was always running around talking about he didn't believe in black power, he just believed in green power, the power of money. But he didn't sell his dope to nobody green, just black people.

"Brother Lonnie." Ugly came over to me and gave me five. "First time I seen you in about five years you ain't got a ball in your hand."

"No big thing," I said. "Say, you seen Paul?"

"I ain't seen my man for about a week now," Ugly said. "He into that ball thing too, ain't he?"

"Yeah, he into it," I said. "What you got in the way of some extra dust over here?"

"Well, what you need, youngblood?"

"I need a pull," I said. "It don't have to be too heavy. You know, something like Paul got."

"That's safe," Ugly said, "but it ain't that tough. He got to be messing with the Big Man's boxes, and if the Big Man catch you, you know you gonna catch some calendar space. Plus I can't let him have but fifteen dollars a digit 'cause there's just too much paper floating around. If you be needing dust, it's angel dust that's pulling in the bucks."

I told him I didn't like to mess with no angel dust because too many heads was messing with it. He said that was the chance I had to take.

I called the club to see if Mary-Ann was there and she was and I told her to meet me over at the Grant. She said okay. On the way over I tried to piece together what was going down. Paul was snatching them checks and selling them to Ugly for fifteen dollars apiece. But I couldn't figure out why Tyrone was getting them. The only thing I could figure was that Paul was snatching them for Tyrone. But if he was doing that, why was Ugly involved in the thing? None of it made any sense, and I didn't want to talk to Mary-Ann until I could say something. So instead of going into the Grant, I turned around when I got to the corner and went over to the center.

There was a little three-on-three action going down, and I got in and busted the first game I played. I was playing against this sucker from Milbank who swore he was bad. Everything I threw up dropped in. I was so bad I surprised myself. When I moved, my feet hardly touched the ground, and when I shot the ball, it didn't touch the rim, just dropped through the net. I was getting that soft shot, like Cal. I tried his move, putting the ball up with one hand off the dribble. A chick that was watching screamed when she saw me do it, and I nearly grinned myself to death. Cal had told me I was nice, but even I didn't know I was this nice.

Another game went by, starring and directed by me, and then I decided to book. I was about to leave when I see Paul come in the other way. I called him over and told him I wanted to see him in our room. He didn't say nothing; he just followed me on in. Ox was in the room, feeding Sparrow, and I asked him to split.

"Y'all gonna do the thing?" he asked.

"Get out of here, man," I said.

"Hey, brother, you know what I say." Ox had put Sparrow back in his cage and was going out the door. "A chick is slick, but gay is okay!"

When Ox left, I closed the door and locked it, and then I asked Paul what was going on. He asked me what I meant.

"What I mean?" I looked at him like he was crazy or something. "You go around punching out some chick you don't even know, you acting funny, you don't say nothing to nobody. Unless you talking to your new la-di-da people."

"What are you? The FBI?"

"I'm just asking, brother."

"If I feel this big need to talk to somebody about what I'm doing, I'll go to confession," he said. "In the meantime, why don't you just walk down your side of the street and I'll walk down mine? Okay?"

"Look, man—"

"Look, nothing, save your looks for a peep show," he said. "I told you I don't want to hear what you got to say."

"Hey, man, I ain't that chick you punched out. If you feel froggy, just leap on over here, sucker!"

There were two things I didn't think would ever

happen. One of them was that Paul and me would ever have a serious fight. The other one was that anybody could hit me one time and put me on the floor. At first I thought he had damaged my brain or something because I saw all these little lights and it hurt so much. Then I realized the sucker had hit me with the lamp. I got up and he hit me in the belly and I grabbed him around the waist and lifted him off the floor. I took a few more punches before I could push him away from me.

I was mad at him, but there was still a lot between us, and I didn't really want to hurt him too much. He came at me again, and I tried to just hold him off. Paul wasn't weak. You just didn't hold him off with no one hand. He was swinging with everything he had, like whatever it was that was messing with him he was going to get off on me. I tried to go light on him, but he was kicking my rump. I didn't know he could fight that hard. He came at me again, and I could tell what he was going to do, but I hadn't recovered from the last time he hit me, so all I could do was to try to get my hand up a little to block the blow. It didn't do no good, and I felt myself going down. I didn't even feel where he hit me at all. All I could feel was me going down. It seemed like I was taking my time about it, and I kind of remember trying to look up and see what he was doing as I went down.

I couldn't get my head together for a while. Then I realized I wasn't being hit. I tried shaking my head to get the cobwebs out, but that hurt. It was like in a flick. Me sitting on the floor, kind of watching things happen around me. I figured I'd better get up pretty quick before he came again, but then I heard the sound of crying. It was Paul, he was leaning against the wall, kind of holding on to it, and crying real hard. If I had been mad I stopped, and just wondered what was going on.

I went through my pockets and found some change and went out into the hall to get some sodas. There was a little kid in the hall. He looked at my face and asked me if I had been fighting.

"No," I said, taking the second soda from the machine.

"You always look like that?" he asked.

"Yeah."

"You sure ugly," the kid said.

I went back into the office and closed the door. Paul was still sitting on the floor, and I went over and sat next to him. He looked at me and the Coke I offered him. He took it, and we sat for a long while just drinking the Cokes. Ox knocked on the door, and I opened it and told him to split. He asked me what happened, and I told him to split again.

"You and Paul have a fight?"

"Look, I don't want to talk about it," I said, still standing in the doorway.

"What happened?" He was trying to look over my shoulder.

"Ain't you got no cool, man?"

"No," he said. He didn't either. I finally got him to split by promising him I'd tell him what happened later.

I sat down next to Paul again, and then I asked him if he wanted to talk about it.

"You see me hanging out with Lenny and trying to get into that middle-class thing—"

"You mean that semiwhitey thing?" I said.

"Hey, it ain't about that. It's about getting over, like I said before. You can run it into the ground, and maybe you can deal with who you are better than I can, but that's the way it is."

"Yeah, but you always been my man. How you get into these changes? One day you my ace boon and the next day I don't know you."

"One day my pops came around and asked me if I wanted to go downtown with him." Paul took a deep breath and let it out hard. "I said okay. We went down where he works. It was his day off, and he just wanted to pick up some stuff from his gig. He works in this office building, doing maintenance, little odd jobs. So he went in and picked some stuff up, and his boss was sitting there with two other whiteys and this sister, and he told my father to go out and get some coffee for them. My father said he wasn't working, and this whitey laughed and said he never was. Then he told him what kind of coffee they wanted. That got next to me, you know. I started to speak on it, and he said he used to catch an attitude when he was younger, but he started getting fired from gigs.

"You know what that was like to me? Seeing my father going for coffee and everything? Because you don't think about going for coffee for nobody. You thinking about yourself fixing something or sitting in an office, that kind of thing. You don't think about being a grown man and fetching coffee for nobody. It was like I was looking over a mountain and seeing where I was going for the first time. You want more soda?"

"No," I said.

"I'm sorry about the fight, man," Paul said.

"Go on about that other stuff," I said.

"I ain't much different than my pops. I kept on trying to tell myself that I was, you know, but I'm not. He's no dummy, man. But he don't have that piece of paper. Anyway, then I met Lenny and Joni, and they were like . . . what? Different, I guess. Yeah, they were la-di-da niggers, just like you said they were. But you know Lenny ain't going to be going for nobody's coffee, man. You just know that. And Joni's going to be the chick sitting up with them whiteys telling somebody like me what kind of coffee they want. I know that. Anyway, I started to hang with them.

"Then one day I was over to Joni's house and I was smoking some joints that Lenny had picked up. I fell off to sleep or something, and when I woke up, Joni and this chick she hangs with sometime—"

"Skinny chick?"

"No, a gray chick," Paul said. "They're out on the balcony—"

"They got a balcony?"

"Yeah, they got a nice place," he said. "Anyway, they out there talking about me and this gray chick is asking Joni if she really digs me and Joni starts going on like that's the biggest joke in the world. She says she just hangs with me sometime because she sees it as a chance to understand ghetto people."

"You should have busted her nose for her," I said. "And then busted that gray chick's nose, too. Nothing them la-di-da niggers hate worse than you putting them down in front of their ace whiteys."

"Yeah, maybe. But that's not how I felt. I felt like

I wanted to prove something, you know. Like I was okay for her to like maybe. Hey, if a black chick who's into something don't dig me, and I'm trying to get away from a certain kind of thing . . . I don't know. So I start taking her out more and buying her things. I didn't have no dust, so I took some checks from the mailbox in that building over the bank."

"Welfare people live in that building."

"Yeah, some," Paul said. "A friend told me. He delivers mail in that building, and he told me that some people there get welfare even though it's supposed to be a high-rent place. I was over there one time and I saw that they hadn't put the mailbox in right and everybody was supposed to be going to the post office for their mail. Even when they started putting the mail in the boxes, the boxes would open if you hit against them."

"So you ripped off the checks and took them to Ugly's," I said.

"How you know that?"

"Because Ugly told me," I said. "I was over there and he asked me if I had seen you and I asked why and he said 'cause he could use some more digits."

"Yeah," Paul said. "Only Tyrone found out about it and said that a friend of his who's a postal inspector was on to the whole thing and they were waiting for me to cop some more checks before they picked me up. He said they knew who I was and everything because somebody had spotted me. So he got the checks from Ugly, and he burned them up so they wouldn't have any evidence."

"He *burned* them?"

"Yeah, that way the only way they can bust me is to catch me copping some more checks, and there's no way I'm going to do that." Paul straightened his legs in front of him and rubbed his left knee. If he hurt it when we were fighting, I hoped it hurt like hell because my face was beginning to pound like I had a toothache.

"So he did you a favor and now you beating up women for him?" I said.

"Not because he did me a favor," Paul said. "He had to buy the checks from Ugly, and I'm doing this to pay him back. He said I'm even now."

"And he burned all the checks?"

"Yeah."

"Why you think he doing this for you, man?" I asked.

"I think because he likes Mary-Ann."

"Yeah, I guess so."

"Say, look, don't tell nobody nothing about this," Paul said. "All I want to do for the rest of the summer is to play some ball and forget what happened."

"Yeah."

After we rapped a little more, I went back over to the Grant. It was a heavy trip, what it was. I could get next to what Paul was saying about his pops because I felt the same way. I didn't think about it all the time, but I did think about it some of the time. In another way I had even thought about trying to be like Lenny and Joni, but every time I saw a black cat acting like that, it made me disgusted. In a way they were always out for coffee.

Paul didn't know that Tyrone hadn't burned the

checks, and I didn't tell him. I called Mary-Ann, listened to her mouth about why I hadn't met her before when I said I would, and then told her not to talk to Paul about what we had done. I told her it was important that she didn't, and she asked me why. I told her what Paul had said and that we'd better try to get all the pieces together before we did any more talking. She said cool on that. Funny that she should be Paul's younger sister because she seemed a lot older in the head than he did.

I went down and got a pint of wine and went back up to my room and drank it. Then I fell asleep and had this dream. I was playing ball for all these scouts. They were all white, and they weren't sitting in *stands* or anything, but they were sitting around the edges of the court. And each one had two la-di-da niggers sitting with them, drinking champagne out of these little plastic champagne glasses. I was playing against about ten other guys, and we were all breaking our butts. Nobody was on teams. It was every man for himself. Whatever basket you took a rebound from, you had to go shoot at the other basket, and everybody was trying to stop you. And all the while we were playing, we kept looking on the sidelines to see if the scouts were digging us, and the la-di-da niggers kept getting up in the faces of the white scouts and smiling and carrying on so they couldn't see us.

When everybody that was playing saw that the scouts couldn't see us, they started carrying the ball and elbowing, and it really got to be a free-for-all. Guys were punching and trying to thumb cats in the eye and stuff like that. Every time a cat would fall down, everybody would come over to where he had fallen and stomp on him and chant until he was wasted and then go on with the game. Then there was just two players left, me and Snakeskin. I didn't even know Snakeskin had been in the game. It had just seemed that there were people without faces, just black arms and black legs and the brown ball. Now it was me and Snakeskin, and the score was tied. I brought the ball down, dribbling through the piles of bodies, and Snakeskin was on my case. I was almost trapped between Snakeskin and a pile of bodies when suddenly I remembered the move that Cal had shown me. Down the right side, around the bodies, and then up in the air off the dribble for the slam!

When I did that, Snakeskin fell to the ground, and I went over and stomped him until he was still. Then I still had to score three more baskets before the game was over. But there wasn't anybody to stop me now, and I could show off my stuff. Only the scouts couldn't see me for the la-di-da niggers in their faces. I went over to the sidelines.

"Here I go!" I shouted. But all you could hear was those la-di-das teheeing and those glasses hitting against each other. I scored one basket, then another.

"Look at me!" I was shouting. "Look at me!"

But they didn't look. I took the ball and ran up to one of the la-di-das and slammed the ball into her head, and she just turned and kept laughing.

She laughed until I woke up.

6

Cal called us together for practice the next day. We all met at the center and went down together, all except Breeze. Cal called his house, but his mother said he had left already.

We took the A train, and all the way downtown Cal was talking to me about Aggie. How she was such a good singer. How fine she was, stuff like that. I didn't really want to hear any of it, though. I *knew* all that stuff already.

"Why you leave her?" I asked.

"I guess I just wasn't together enough for her," he said.

I didn't know what that meant, but he wasn't talking anymore, so I let it lay.

When we got to the gym, Breeze was already there. He was selling cassettes to some of the kids in the summer program. He was always selling something to kids. I told him that the reason he sold to kids all the time was because he was just about on their mental level.

"What we're going to work on today," Cal said, "is Mr. Calvin Jones's TIT."

"It sounds better than Gatorade," Roy said, and everybody cracked on that.

"I guess it does," Cal said. "It always sounds good before practice starts. Now the TIT is simple. TIT stands for Two-Inch Theory. If you can jump two inches more than the guy you jumping against, you going to beat him. You don't have to jump a foot more, just two inches. If you can get two inches on a man when you driving, you can score on him.

"If you can get two inches on a man when you going for a loose ball, you're going to get the ball. And to get all these two inches, you have to try a little harder than what you think your best is right now. Do we all understand what Mr. Jones is talking about, girls?"

Everybody said they understood, and then we made some more cracks about tits and stuff, and then Cal had us all stand near the top of the key. He got a ladder and put it next to the backboard. Then he covered the hoop with a board and Scotch taped some paper to the backboard. One by one we had to come over to the backboard and jump up and touch the paper as high as we could, and then he marked where we touched and put our names next to it.

Roy got up the highest; I came in second; then Ox, Breeze, Paul, and Lenny. Jo-Jo, Walter, and the rest of the scrubs did okay, but not as good as the starters. Then Cal made each of us go to a basket and put a piece of tape on the backboard as high as we had jumped on the first board.

"Now all I want you to do is to jump two inches higher than that mark and you can sit down and have a soda on me and then we can play some four-on-four."

It sounded easy enough. Roy started in first, but Cal stopped him and called him over to where he was standing under the board.

"Now do it!" Cal said.

Roy jumped up but missed the tape. He tried again. He missed again. Then he backed off and started to come in, but Cal stopped him.

"No good," he said. "I want you to come in and start from here."

We had been had. When he first told us to come and make the jump, we had been standing at the top of the key, so naturally we had started out with a run so we could really sky. Now we were trying to jump from a standstill.

"You keep jumping now," Cal said, "until you're ready to go show me how you can go two inches over that tape. You just yell out 'TIT,' and I'll come running over."

Everybody really tried hard at first, but none of us could make it. Then we started slipping further away from the tape as we got tired. Every time we tried to catch some rest, Cal would come over and get on our cases. We called a few things out, but none of them had anything to do with two inches.

I had come to the practice ready to show Cal that I wanted to take care of business. When he talked about his Two-Inch Theory, it was cool with me because I was ready to do it. I figured I would show him that I could work harder than anybody else. But the practice wasn't hard, it was ridiculous. He had us jumping until I swear I could hear my heart beating louder in my ears than anything else. Then he had us scrambling around on the floor for balls. Not once or twice, but for a half hour! For the whole half hour nobody could stand on his feet. I asked him who he thought we were going to be playing, the NBA All-Stars?

When the practice was finally over, nobody said a word. That's how tired we were. I wanted to talk to Cal about what had went down with Paul, but I didn't want Paul to know I was rapping about his situation. I hadn't spoken to him any more about it, and Mary-Ann said that she didn't even talk to him about it.

We took showers and were getting dressed, still without talking, when Matt Lee came in with this old dude. He wasn't really that old, but he was just about bald. He was from a black newspaper and wanted to take some pictures and interview some of the guys. Cal said he could interview some of the guys if he wanted to, but no flicks. That was a downer because everybody wanted to get their flick in the paper. If he had put all our pictures in the paper, they wouldn't have to sell them on the newsstands because we would have bought them all.

Anyway, Cal didn't go for it, and that was that. I dug him pulling Matt Lee over to the side and talking to him, and then Lee took the newspaper guy out. When everybody was leaving, I asked Cal if he wanted to see another play I had worked out, and he said okay. I did have another play, but that was really just an excuse to talk to him. We went out in the bright afternoon light carrying our bags, and some Puerto Rican kids asked us if we were basketball players. I said yeah, we were.

"Can I have your autograph?" the kid asked, pushing a comic book toward me.

"I ain't really nobody famous," I said.

"You going to be somebody famous?" he asked.

"He sure is," Cal said.

"Then give me your autograph, and I'll save it for later," he said. I signed the edge of the comic book, and then I had to sign another autograph for another little Puerto Rican girl with eyes that were just about ready to break some dude's heart.

"Kids are something else," Cal said.

"How come you never had kids?" I asked.

"I had a child," he said.

I stopped in my tracks. This guy was getting to be like a hole in the ground that you couldn't see the bottom of. The deeper you reached, the deeper the dude went. He walked on a few steps ahead of me and then turned around.

"You coming, or you going to spend the rest of the afternoon standing there posing on the sidewalk?"

"Where's your kid?" I asked. "I know it's got to be a girl. That's why you don't want her around me, afraid I might take advantage of her, right?"

"No, a boy, Jeffrey," Cal said. "He'd be younger than you now."

The way he said that I knew the kid was dead. I really felt bad about it, too. Looked like wherever I reached into the man I came out with a handful of pain.

"Sorry, man," I said. I figured I would say that and then shut up unless he wanted to talk about it.

"You know, I got a call from this guy O'Donnel who's sponsoring the tournament," Cal said. "He said he wants to see me about something tomorrow. The tournament's a little bigger than some people thought it would be. They picked up some commercial sponsors, soft drink people, a tire company."

"That's good, ain't it?" I asked.

"Yeah, real good, in a way," Cal said. "You want to stop for a soda?"

I said yes and we stopped in Whelan's on Eighth Avenue. I ordered a chicken salad on toast and a milk shake, and Cal ordered a Coke. I was pretty sure the waitress had eyes for me. I mentioned it to Cal.

"People see in you what they need," he said. "You got to be what *you* need."

"She's still fine," I said.

"That's 'cause you got more nature than taste," he said, smiling. It was the first time that he had smiled since we left the school. I could tell something was on his mind, but I didn't know what.

"You really think we have a chance in this tournament?" I asked.

"We got a good chance," he answered. "You want to come with me when I go to see O'Donnel tomorrow?"

"Yeah."

"I guess you got a jacket and tie?"

"Sure I do," I said. "What do I look like?"

"Just checking," he said. "After we see O'Donnel, we can come down here and let that waitress check you out in your jacket."

"She may not be able to take the whole thing at one time," I said.

"You know . . ." He started talking but stopped when the waitress brought our order. I looked her in the eye, and she smiled at me. I figured maybe I would drop by in my jacket. When she left the table, Cal started talking again. "They had about three hearings when I was brought up on charges for shaving points. The first meeting was with the commissioner's office. Then I had another meeting with the district attorney, and then another with the commissioner. What it all came down to was that the commissioner worked out a deal where I didn't have to do no time and the gamblers I was dealing with didn't have to do no time. I got a four-month suspended sentence, and the gambler he got a six-month suspended sentence. Well, it didn't mean nothing to him because he didn't have no reputation to protect or nothing.

"Me, I was out the NBA, I didn't have a job, and I didn't have nothing to turn to. Aggie had stopped singing, more or less, and was home with the baby. He was about three. She had thought she might try again when Jeff got older, but right then she was okay just being home. She read the stories in the papers about me being involved in an investigation, and she asked me what was going on. Well, at the start of the whole thing the team put it out that I had pulled a groin muscle, and I'd be out for at least a week. That's how they covered it. So I told her that was what the thing was, this injury. It worked out pretty good, too. I told her I couldn't do nothing at night because it hurt. I was so worried about what was going to happen.

"Then they dropped it on me. I got a ten-thousand-dollar fine and a promise of a suspended sentence if I didn't make any waves. Other than that, they said I'd have to go to jail.

"We were playing, at least the team was playing, in St. Louis when I came home and told Aggie what happened. She just didn't believe it. She looked at me like she didn't even know me. Then, when I had finished running all the details down to her, she looked at me and said, 'What are we going to do now?'

"The ten thousand dollars was more than we had saved. We had to borrow some money. Couldn't even borrow it at first. Then I went to the same guy that messed me up—that had let me mess myself up. I told him that I didn't have the money to pay the fine. I needed three thousand dollars more. He lent it to me, at twenty percent interest."

"He should have given you the money!" I said.

"Why?" Cal looked up at me. "He didn't have no more use for me!"

"I'd have wasted the sucker!"

"Yeah, then I would have been in jail. Anyway, Aggie got a job working in a factory down on Varick

Street. I couldn't find nothing. I was staying home with Jeffrey and feeling sorry for myself. It got so that I didn't want people to see me in the street. I wore dark glasses and let my beard grow. People used to ask me what happened, and I'd say they chumped me off so they could let some white boy on the team. Then one day I heard about this job with a paper company. I asked this girl to look after Jeffrey. I only had a dollar to give her. She wasn't much, but I thought if I could get the job and make it last a week, we'd have enough money so that Aggie could stay home. I didn't say nothing to Aggie. The job wasn't that far away, and I could leave after her and get back home before her. The fourth day, the day before payday, I come home and the street is full of fire engines.

"I knew. Nobody didn't have to tell me nothing. I knew. We got home from the funeral, and I told Aggie I was going. She didn't say nothing. She just sat there near the window in front of the crib. We had been looking at beds, you know, the kind with the rails on the side? But we hadn't got one yet. Aggie just sat there, and I just walked out."

We finished our order and went out to the subway. By that time I didn't feel like telling Cal nothing about Paul. On the way uptown he asked me how I felt about the team's offense, and I said I thought it was okay. He told me that it had one problem.

"What's that?"

"It's got to have a leader," he said. "You know what I mean?"

I nodded.

* * *

That night I went over to my moms's place and picked up my suit. It looked okay. I took it over to the Grant. When I got there, Mary-Ann was waiting in the lobby, rapping with Harrison.

"You have quite a young lady here," Harrison said.

"I know," I said. "She so fine I moved her up from number seven all the way up to number four on my list."

I gave Harrison a wink and took Mary-Ann on upstairs. I asked her if Tyrone had said anything about his place being busted into. He hadn't.

"I don't really understand it," she said. "Veronica said that when he found out about it, he was really mad, but he hasn't blown his top. He talked about taking care of it when Juno got back."

"Who's Juno?" I asked.

"You know that big dude who hangs around the place? Always blinking when he looks at you?"

"Got them big ham hands?"

"Yeah, that freak," Mary-Ann said. "You can't be leaving no clothes around or he'll have them. Especially shoes, he's a freak for ladies' shoes. He's either doing that or beating people's heads in. Tyrone uses him as a bouncer sometimes and as a bodyguard."

"He ain't got no idea who did it, so how's he going to take care of it when Juno gets back?" I asked.

"Veronica thinks he knows who did it," Mary-Ann said. "I've been thinking about quitting, but I don't want to quit until this thing is over so he won't think I had anything to do with it."

"Yeah, if Juno was to mess with you, I'd have to blow his fat, greasy butt away."

"You'd have to get you a silver bullet and shoot him through the heart," Mary-Ann said. "Either that or burn his coffin when he's out sucking blood."

"How you like my suit?" I asked. "Want me to try it on for you?"

"No."

"No? Why not?"

"Because I want to talk to you about something," she said. She sat on the end of the bed and lay back. She was looking good. I hadn't really noticed that she was getting kind of chesty, but she was. Not too much, but enough.

"What you want to talk about?" I said, sitting on the bed next to her and putting my hand on her knee.

"Us," she said, pushing my hand away. "What are we all about?"

"You know I dig you," I said.

"Well, what does that mean?" she said, looking at me upside down. "You want to marry me?"

"*Marry* you?"

"You ain't never heard that word before?" she said. "It's marry, you know, *m* like in marry, *a* like in marry, *r* like in—"

"Yeah, I know what you talking about."

"You mad?"

"Lighten up!"

"That's a real turnoff, huh?" she said. "Really puts your nature down, don't it?"

"Where is all this coming from anyway?" I said.

"Look how mad you're getting!" she said.

"Hey, I ain't getting mad, so just cut it!"

"Now just for that I'm really going to get you mad,"

she said. She sat up and spun around and came up with this hard-looking face. "Lonnie Jackson, I love you! I love everything about you! I know it makes you mad, but I don't care. I love the way you walk, Lonnie Jackson, I love the way you comb your hair! How's that?"

"Lighten up, chick," I said.

"I love the way you kiss and the way you stretch in the morning!" she went on.

"Come on and knock it off, you're getting worse than Cal."

"Cal's in love with you?" She stopped and looked at me.

"No, that's not what I mean," I said. "I mean—"

I didn't know what I meant. I snatched my jacket and went on downstairs. I felt crowded in, like I was suffocating or something.

1

O'Donnel's office was really nice. It was on Fifty-seventh Street just off Madison Avenue. It was funny, because his office didn't have a desk in it. When his secretary told me and Cal to go in, she did say go into his office, but it looked like somebody's living room.

"Cal Jones, good to see you, good to see you." O'Donnel was young-looking, but his hair was all white. He was wearing a gray suit and a soft blue shirt that was open at the collar. The hair on his chest was white, too, and I figured that's why he wore his shirt open, to show it off.

"Mr. O'Donnel, this is Lonnie Jackson," Cal said.

I shook hands with Mr. O'Donnel, and he said something about being pleased to meet me and all. Then we sat down. O'Donnel sat in a chair near a table, and Cal and I sat on a sofa. The sofa was one of these real soft numbers so that you sink all the way down. I really wanted to stand, but I figured it wasn't cool.

"What do you think of the tournament, Cal?" O'Donnel said, leaning back in his chair.

"I think it's a good opportunity for the young people involved," Cal said. "Anytime that they have the chance to show off their skills in front of college scouts, it's going to be good for them."

"I agree with you," O'Donnel said. He reached over and opened a box and took out two cigars and offered one to Cal. Cal shook his head no, and then O'Donnel did his cigar. First he sniffed it; then he took a little pair of scissors from his pocket and cut the end off; then he lit it. All the time me and Cal is sitting there, waiting for him to finish.

I take a look over Cal, and I see he's twisting his hands and I figured that he was as uncomfortable as I was. It was as if O'Donnel was sitting there letting us remember where our place was. I felt myself wishing I had bought myself a new shirt or had on something new so I wouldn't feel as small as I was feeling. When O'Donnel finally got around to talking again, I was glad—and I think he knew it, too.

"You know what worries me, Cal?" O'Donnel said. "That this tournament is going to become a one-time thing. The sponsors look at it this year and say, 'Unh-unh, no more,' and that's very easy for them to do. The money they're investing is not important money.

Hoops

The total investment is maybe one hundred to one hundred and fifty thousand dollars. They're giving away a few sets of sneakers, renting the courts, doing a little promotional work, nothing big. But that's not the problem. The problem is that they spend millions of dollars in advertising away from the tournament, and anything that gives them a black eye is going to eat into those millions. You know what I mean?"

"I don't see why the tournament should give anybody a black eye," Cal said.

"Well, it's easy. You get a couple of kids drinking, or fighting, and in comes the newspapers. I can see the headline: 'Coaches' Tournament Kids Fight!' The newspapers will have a field day with something like that."

"I think you're overplaying the whole thing," Cal said. "In the first place, it's not called the Coaches' Tournament; it's being called the Tournament of Champions. They've set up minitournaments all over the city, and the champions from each minitournament will be in the tournament that is sponsored. The others aren't even sponsored. And you either believe in these kids or you don't."

"I agree with you there, Cal," O'Donnel said—he was using his cigar like a pointer. "That's why I want to be very careful and ward off any possible problems. I mean a kid can do something and not understand the kind of trouble it might lead to. Hell, man, you of all people should know about that."

"Yeah, well, is that the point?" Cal asked.

"The point is just to avoid trouble," O'Donnel said.

"What's it got to do with us?" I asked.

111

"From what I've heard, you're one of the teams that will probably make the Finals," O'Donnel said to me. "And, as I'm sure that Cal has told you, he's had some trouble in the past. What I want to know is how we're going to handle any adverse publicity if it does occur."

"How did you hear about our team?" Cal asked. "And how did you know I was coaching the team?"

"Let's just put it this way," O'Donnel said, blowing a puff of smoke towards the ceiling, "let's just say I have my sources."

Cal didn't say anything, and I didn't say anything. O'Donnel just kept puffing on his cigar and looking at it like he had never seen one before. This went on for a while, and then Cal asked O'Donnel what he thought we should do.

"That's up to you, of course," O'Donnel said. "If you think you should withdraw as coach . . . well, I could understand it. My primary interest is in the kids. In Lonnie here, for example."

"Who your sources that don't dig Cal?" I asked.

"I'm not at liberty to reveal that information," O'Donnel said.

"What we got to do," I said to Cal, "is to tell the newspapers that this white cat doesn't want us in the tournament."

"I didn't say that," he said. "The only thing I said is that there has been some information . . ."

"How do you know your information is right?" Cal said. "How do you know the person supplying your information is straight? Because if he isn't, then you might have a lot more problems than you think you have," Cal said. He stood up and started towards the door.

O'Donnel jumped up and cut him off.

"Look, Cal," he said. "I don't want trouble for anybody. The only thing I want to do is see that the kids get what is coming to them, and that's a chance to show off their skills. Is that too much to ask?"

"Either one of two things is going to happen," Cal said. "Either you're going to get me the name of your source or I'm going to the black press to find out why you're trying to give this tournament a bad name!"

"*I'm* trying . . . ?" O'Donnel looked at Cal like he didn't believe him. "Wait a minute."

He went over to the table he had been sitting at before and pulled out the drawer. There were buttons on the drawer, and he pressed one. A moment later the secretary came in with her notebook and a pencil. That was definitely cool. He told her to bring him the file on the tournament.

"What's your stake in this anyway?" Cal said.

"What stake?" O'Donnel said. He was putting out his cigar, and I figured the lead had just changed hands.

"I'm only going to ask you one more time," Cal said. He took a step closer to O'Donnel and there was fear all over the guy.

"My firm handles public relations," O'Donnel said. "Handling this won't hurt us, maybe it'll even help us in a small way with some of the accounts involved."

The secretary returned with the file, and O'Donnel went back over to his table and pulled the chair around to the back of it and sat down.

"There was a phone call from a Mr. Rashid. That's R-A-S-H-I-D," O'Donnel said.

"Yeah," Cal answered, "we'll keep the name in mind."

"Who's Rashid?" I asked after we had got outside. Cal didn't know.

"Then who the hell is O'Donnel?" I asked.

"O'Donnel is what basketball is all about," Cal said. "O'Donnel and cats like him. Because what it's all about is people paying to come into the gym and people paying to put their ads on television. He ain't saying I can't coach good; he's saying I might hurt that money the sponsors are putting up.

"First thing a guy like O'Donnel does when he sets up a tournament is find out who can win and how they going to look to somebody who's got some money to put up. Cats putting up big money to sell soft drinks don't want no jailbirds on the court. They don't want nobody with no dirt on them. And no matter how clean you look, they're going to bend over backwards to look even cleaner. He's got scouts telling him who can win, and somebody's whispered our name in the man's ears."

I tried to talk to him some more about it, but it wasn't getting through too tough. It had got to Cal, I could tell. The way he was acting and everything, like he was tired. Cal was never tired. He could play ball with us and then run laps and look better than we did.

I didn't dig O'Donnel telling us what to do and playing his little game. When I left Cal, I told him to forget what O'Donnel had said. He told me to remember it.

"Why I want to remember that crap?" I asked.

"Because you got to make a decision," Cal said. "That's why I brought you along. I sort of thought that would be the story."

"I already made my decision," I told him. "You coach."

I went over to the center to tell the other guys. I found them arguing on the corner about if Superman could fly or was he just jumping around.

"Dig it," Ox was saying, "they say he can leap tall buildings with a single bound. They didn't say nothing about him *flying* no tall buildings!"

"Ox, where do you keep your brain, man?" Paul said.

"They say, 'Look! Up in the sky! It's a bird! It's a plane! No, it's Superman!' Now do they say that or do they not say that?"

"Yeah, they said it," Ox said, "but they didn't say how he got up in the sky."

"They put him with a bird and a plane, man!" Paul said. "You ever see a bird leap? You ever see a plane leap? No, they're flying and Superman is flying, too! That is why he wears that cape, to help him keep himself stabilized!"

"He wears that cape because that's the cape his daddy gave him to wear," Ox said. "Didn't you see the picture?"

"How come he got to wear an *S* on his chest, man?" Jo-Jo asked.

"In case he forget his name?"

"We got to have a meeting," I said. "Let's go into the office and rap."

"About Superman?"

I ignored Paul, and we went on into the center. Ox had the keys out, but he saw the door was open.

"Oh, man!" Ox stopped dead in his tracks. "Oh, no!"

I pushed by Ox and looked in. The place was a shambles. Everything that had been standing had been thrown over. The pictures we had on the wall were torn down. The record player was broken, and the records were all over the floor. You could see the heel marks on the records that weren't broken. All the drawers had been taken out of the old desk we had and thrown on the floor. Ox, standing next to me, pushed out one foot and lifted a torn record cover. Under it was Sparrow, his parakeet.

"Oh, man . . . oh, man . . ." Ox knelt on the pile of records and gently lifted the dead bird. He held it in his two hands and looked down at it like he didn't believe what he saw. "Oh, man . . . I ain't never had nothing living before. I ain't even had a plant or nothing that really lived . . ."

In Ox's huge black hands the dead bird looked like a child's feather toy. The tears were running down his face, and his mouth was open as if there were things to say he just couldn't get out. I felt sorry for him, and at the same time I was wondering how it was that a guy as big as Ox had something so fragile to hold onto. I was sorry for the dude, and ashamed of the way he just broke down.

We looked for places to put our eyes, but the sound

of Ox's crying, softer now than it was, kept pulling us back to him. I caught Paul's eyes for a moment, and we both looked away from each other quickly. The whole thing was too close to us, too real, and too intimidating to let on that we even knew about it.

"Must have been a junkie," Paul said.

"A junkie ain't got the time to be doing all this," I said. "Whoever was here took his damn time. He wanted to hurt us."

"Why he want to hurt us?" Walter was pushing through the stuff with his foot.

"I don't know," I said. "But for some simple dudes like us there's sure a lot of stuff going on."

"Like what?" Paul asked.

I didn't answer. I leaned against the wall and watched as Ox put Sparrow in a box. Some of the other guys started to clean up a little and then just said, "The hell with it." It wasn't worth it. Breeze got all his cassettes together even though they were broken. That was cool, and I started to get my stuff up, but then I didn't feel like it.

Finally I told them that I had been up to O'Donnel's place and how he had said that he didn't want Cal to be the coach because he didn't dig Cal. Everybody said, "Later," for O'Donnel. I left it at that.

We played five games in three days against the other teams in our tournament. We won all five, too. The team wasn't playing that together, but we were still kicking rump. When we played the last game, Cal told us to imagine that we were twenty points behind from the get-go and that we had to make a comeback. We won by six points, and Cal chewed us out. He said it was a raggedy game. Most of us knew it was, but we had won. That was the important thing.

Mary-Ann was coming to the games, but she was being different. I couldn't say nothing to her that she wanted to hear. Still, I wanted her to be around.

Cal started us back into the practice thing again, which didn't go down too cool. Everybody said we would really get down to business when the Tournament of Champions started. Cal was pushing a little too hard. Everybody wanted to win, but he was acting like he was going to be playing instead of us. Ox told him that, too.

"You guys ain't men enough to play with me," he said. He laid it down like he meant it, too. A couple of cats caught attitudes behind that, and the practices tailed off again.

I was getting too many things on my mind. Everywhere I turned there was something to worry about. I kept on telling myself to cool out, but it wasn't happening. I rapped a little to Mary-Ann about it and that helped some, and I dug on how much I was getting out of being with her and telling her what was on my mind. I hadn't told her about Cal getting into trouble before. I guess I didn't want her to think anything bad about the dude, but finally it came out. I had taken her to a flick, and we were waiting for the train at Forty-deuce.

"Me and Cal went up to see one of the tournament directors last week," I said. "He was trying to give Cal some static about something he did a long time ago."

"What he do?" she asked.

"He got accused of shaving points," I said, hoping it didn't sound so bad.

"Is that cheating?" she asked.

"What you mean, 'cheating'?" I asked.

"You don't know what cheating means?"

"Yeah, he was cheating," I said. "Anyway, some dude named Russia or Rassha or something like that called this whitey and told him."

"Rashid?" She looked at me sideways. "He called?"

"Yeah, you know him?"

The train came and we got on. It was crowded, and we got separated. We had to wait until 125th Street before the train emptied enough so we could get back together.

"That's Juno's last name. Or the name he goes by anyway," she said. "Juno Rashid. First his name was Juno Brown. Then he changed it to Abdul Rashid. But everybody kept calling him Juno, so then he just called himself Juno Rashid."

"He know Cal?" I asked.

"How I know who he knows?" Mary-Ann said.

I took Mary-Ann home and then called Cal's place, and he didn't answer. Sometimes he had been staying over with Aggie. I figured they were getting back together again or something. I looked in the telephone book under "A. Jones," but I couldn't find her number. Information said she had a number, but it wasn't listed.

"I want to run through a series of plays today," Cal was saying when I got to the gym. "So that we can change from one play into the next without bringing the ball back outside to the top of the key. The first play will be from the top, and then the second will be from the corner."

I asked Cal if I could speak to him about something for a minute, and he said I could when we took a break. That ticked me off, and I gave him a look so he would know I had something important to run down. He still didn't seem to dig it, so I went on with the plays. The plays were boss, but my heart wasn't in it. I thought we were never going to take a break, but we finally did. Soon as he said, "Break," everybody slumped to the floor except me. I went over to Cal.

"Now, what was his name first?" he asked when I told him about what Mary-Ann had said.

"First it was Juno Brown," I said. "Then he switched it to Abdul Rashid and then Juno Rashid."

"How do you know this is the guy that called O'Donnel?"

"How I know?" I looked at him. "I don't know that this is the guy, but how many guys out here you know named Rashid and know anything about our team?"

"How he know about the team?" Cal asked.

I started to tell him that, and he held me up and said we would get together after practice. I couldn't understand why he didn't call the practice off and get on the case. He didn't, though, and we worked the rest of the morning on plays.

"Tomorrow night we have our first game," he said. "This is the round-robin part of the tournament. From now on there's going to be scouts in the crowds checking you out. Remember four things. . . ."

He pulled out a piece of paper and started reading from it.

"The first thing is that these coaches know basketball; you're not going to impress them with any sloppy play. The second thing is that they already have their squads at their schools, and they're looking for players who can fit in with their team, not be the team. Third, they're looking for guys with a complete game. That means defense as well as offense. And last, and most important, don't talk to any of them without my permission. I see you talking to anybody that even smells like a scout and I'm putting you on the bench for the next game. Everybody dig that?"

Everybody said that they dug it, and Cal told us to go on home and report back to the gym the next night at six o'clock. I took a quick shower and then found Cal. He was talking to Matt Lee. I waited for him to finish, and then I went up to him. We went across town, and he took me down to Fifty-third Street to the Museum of Modern Art. We walked around there while we talked.

"So how he know about the team?" he said.

"I don't know how he know," I said. "I think he does, though."

"Why?" Cal asked

I ran down the stuff about Paul getting into trouble with the guy who ran the club and that this Rashid character worked for the same guy. All the time I'm rapping Cal is looking at pictures, but I could tell his mind was working overtime. If I even said a word that he didn't get, he would make me go back over it again. I told him all about the checks, how me and Mary-Ann had got them, about Ugly, the whole bit.

"What you know about this guy who runs the club?" Cal asked.

"He thinks he's bad," I said. "Always trying to style, showing off his bread and that kind of thing."

"Is he bad?"

"He don't look that bad to me," I said. "I seen some bad dudes before. Badder than this guy."

"Yeah, and you and Mary-Ann went into his office and took the checks and he didn't say nothing to nobody?"

"No," I said. "And he had to know it was gone because he was only in Chicago for a day, he couldn't have forgot it."

Cal stopped dead in his tracks and looked at me. His face changed so quick I thought he was going off or something. He looked at me for a minute and then walked over to a bench that faced a large painting.

"See this picture?" he said. "It's about the Spanish Civil War."

"If you say so, man," I said.

"This cat from Chicago?" he asked.

"I don't know, but if he paints like that, Chicago must be a weird place!"

"No, man, this Tyrone—what did you say his last name was?"

"I don't know," I said.

"I got a call from some cat named Tyrone something—maybe Tyrone Giddins—wanted to talk to me about the team. He called once or twice and said something about being interested in helping out financially. I just told him to shove off."

He kept on talking to himself. At first he said a few words out loud, and then I could tell he was still talking to himself in his head because every once in a while he would nod to himself. I asked him what he thought it was all about, and he said he didn't know, but he was sure going to try to find out.

The day of the game I woke up nervous. Basketball never made me nervous before. Ox called up about fifteen minutes after I woke up, and he told me he was nervous, too. All right. I knew I had all day to kill, so I went over some of the diagrams of the plays, ran them in my mind until I could see them.

Joni called to wish me luck. I asked her if she was going to wish Paul luck, too.

"I just did," she said. "He's in the shower now."

"In the shower?"

"Um-hm," she whispered into the phone, "I wish it were you, darling. Maybe soon it will be. Good-bye."

She hung up the phone.

Joni knew the kind of things to say. She knew how to say it, too. Even though I knew it was phony, and she knew it was phony, it still got next to me.

The next team we played was half white, so I figured that they couldn't be much. They had this one whitey they called Sweet Jesus who was supposed to hold me. He was about six four and had long hair and a beard. The sucker didn't warm up and spent the whole time before the game with a towel on his head. I told Paul to send out for some soda because I was going to have the sucker's heart for lunch. It didn't quite come off that way.

The first time the fool came downcourt he took me inside, got the ball, and dunked backwards. The next time he got the ball he told me he was going left, was going to stop, and throw in a soft jumper that wasn't going to touch anything but the net and my ego. He did it, too. The fool had me believing he could walk on water by the third quarter. My best game was as good as his, and I think he knew it. I was playing my best game, too, and just wondering whether he was playing his. When I had the ball, he was on my case like a hungry dog on a pork chop. When he had the ball, I was doing everything I knew how to do and the cat was still getting his stuff off.

We won the game, but it brought us back to earth. We were so tired afterwards we couldn't even get off the benches in the locker room. But we had won, by one point.

"If I wasn't so tired," Ox said, "I'd roll over and die."

Cal said that we had played well, that the team we had played against was really good and played much better team ball than we had.

"That cat I was playing was pretty good," I said.

"Pretty good?" Cal laughed. "He's as good as you are, man. You got to learn to play with cats as good as you are and some better. You did okay against him."

Joe Hare, the guy who keeps score at the gym where we play, came over and told me that the white cat had come over to the scoring table after the game and asked what my name was and what school I went to.

"You give him my name?" I asked.

"Sure did," Joe said. "Said you weren't sure what college you were going to, but you were leaning towards the Big Ten."

I grinned a little, I guess. I was glad he had come over and asked about me.

Hoops

Me and Walter were the last ones out of the locker room. We ran into some of the guys from the other team. They said they didn't know the games were going to be that tough. I just shrugged, and Walter said something about the game not being that tough. That made them feel bad. I was a little sorry for them but still glad that it wasn't me feeling bad.

"Which way you going, coach?" I said to Cal, who was standing outside on the corner.

"I'm waiting for a guy who's supposed to pick me up," Cal said. "Why don't you guys go on? You know we got practice in the morning."

Just as we were going off, a car pulled up at the curb.

We went on down the street, still talking about the game. We just couldn't get enough of it. Walter started to say something about how nervous he had been, but he looked back and suddenly stopped talking.

I looked back, too, and saw two guys standing on the corner in front of Cal. They looked like they were arguing, but I couldn't be sure. Then one of them got into a car. The other one opened the back door of the car for Cal, and he got in. He had put his hand on Cal when he was getting in, and I couldn't tell from where I was standing if he had pushed him or not. The car started up, and I stood near the edge of the sidewalk so I could look into it. When it went by me, Cal held up his hand as if everything was all right. Maybe it was.

I went on over to my moms's house, but she wasn't there. I saw one of the neighbors, a skinny chick named Karen who must have been about fifty but who looked like she was thirty, and she said that she had seen my moms in the Spotlite on One-two-five Street. Later for that, I thought, and went over to the Grant. When I got over there, Mary-Ann was sitting in the lobby reading *Ebony*.

"What you doing here?"

"I ain't got nothing else to do," she said.

We went on up to the room I was staying in, and I took a shower. When I got out, the tiredness from the game came down on me. Mary-Ann had some money, so I asked her to go out for some Chinese food.

"I ain't hungry," she said.

"Well, I am," I said.

"Let's go out later."

"How you and your mama been getting along?"

"Why you ask?"

"Because you don't come to the Grant unless you and her have a fight," I said. "That's why."

"We didn't have no fight," Mary-Ann said. She was lying on the bed, kind of halfheartedly going through the *Ebony*. "I just figured I'd come by and see what you were doing."

"Why don't you cop a walk and come back in about an hour and a half so I can cop some rest, baby?" I said. "And why don't you bring some Chinese food with you when you come back? Maybe some shrimp fried rice, or some moo goo gai pan, or even some ribs if your stash can carry it."

"Why don't you just lay yourself on down and rest and then maybe later I'll get up and get the food?" she said. "Unless you're nervous about me being on the bed and all."

"Why not?" I didn't feel like playing with the chick and all, but I lay down on the bed with her. All I had on was some cutoffs I wore around the place sometimes, but I really didn't care too tough, I was so tired.

"Lonnie?"

"What?"

"You like me?"

"What you want me to say?"

"How come you never hit on me?"

"That ain't what we're about," I said.

"What's that mean?"

"You know, we ain't about no bam-bam thing."

"You've had sex with other girls," she said. "You want me to tell you who?"

"Hey, I'm tired."

"Why don't you want me?"

"It's not that I don't want you," I said. "It's got to be different with you. It can't be just—getting some. You know what I mean."

"Make it different," she said. "You want to make it different? Tell me that you love me. Tell me what it means to you, what makes it different."

"How'd we get into this anyway?"

Mary-Ann turned toward me and kissed my chest. I didn't really want her to do that. She just didn't kiss it like she was friendly; she kissed it slow enough for me to feel how soft her lips were and how cool they were against my body. I put my arm around her shoulders.

"The only thing that can make it different is if we make it different for each other," she said. "I love you, that makes it different for me. I want to be your woman. You make it different for me, not just different, more. I just love you so much I can feel you with me even when you're not around. It's like I got you inside me and you keep me warm and do all sorts of good things for me. Can you get next to that feeling? Can you feel anything like it?"

"I can dig it."

"Tell me about it."

"What you want?"

"You loving me."

I kissed her forehead and then her lips. I had been wanting to make love to Mary-Ann for a long time, and I figured I would when the time was right. When she moved against me, I wanted her right then and there.

"Look, can't we wait?" I said.

"Why?" she whispered in my ear.

I slid my hand along the small of her back and down her hips until I was holding the back of her thigh and wondering why myself.

"Because I want it to be different," I said.

"No, you don't." Mary-Ann turned away from me. "The last thing in the world you want is for our making love to be different because the only way it's going to be different is if you make a commitment to me. If you can get out of your head long enough to love somebody."

"Why don't you split?" I said, pulling my arm from around her. "If you just came over here to fight with me, you can leave now."

"Are you afraid to say that you love me?"

"I ain't afraid to say nothing."

"Then say it, Lonnie."

"Why?"

"Do you love me?"

"Yeah, I guess so."

"You *guess* so?"

"I love you," I said, "okay?"

"I didn't hear you," she said. "You're going to have to whisper it very softly into my ear."

She leaned against me gently, and I turned to her and whispered very softly into her ear that I loved her. She got on her knees on the bed and leaned over me and whispered into my ear that she loved me. Then she turned her ear again to my lips, and I whispered that I loved her, and some other things, and kissed her. I held her for a while, and we kissed as she undressed. I told her again that I loved her as the neon sign from the cut-rate liquor store across the street turned the dirty shade a bright orange.

Afterwards I felt good and bad about what had happened. Mary-Ann had been wrong when she said that I didn't want to make it different because I didn't want to make a commitment to her. I did want to love her, to have her for my woman, but it wasn't easy. I had been holding back for so long that I wasn't sure if I could love her or anyone else. I looked at her, the sheets twisted about her body as she slept, and knew that I loved her more than anything that I had ever loved before. I wanted to tell her how much I loved her, to let her know how much I felt for her, but I wasn't sure I could. But I knew, somehow, that I would have to if I wanted her to love me.

I kissed her, and still sleeping, she smiled.

* * *

When Cal didn't show for practice the next morning, I was disappointed and nervous. I tried to get some enthusiasm in the practice, but it didn't come. When he didn't show for the next couple of days, I felt myself pushing the panic button. We played one game without Cal and lost to a mediocre team from Staten Island that we should have beaten easily. When I saw how the guys were acting, how down they were, I knew that they had put a lot of faith in Cal the same way that I had. The tournament didn't mean as much without someone to play for, without Cal.

I went around to just about everywhere I thought Cal should be. I looked in every place he ever mentioned to me. I even hung one whole night outside his place to see if he came around. He didn't.

I called Aggie, she sounded like she didn't care if he was around or not. I asked her if she had seen him, and she said no. That's all, just no. Then I asked her if he had said anything to her about where he might be. She asked me if I thought she was the FBI or something. I went over to Aggie's place anyway, mainly because I didn't know what else to do.

I sat on her stoop after she didn't answer the bell. It was cool, and the clouds were making it darker than it should have been for the time of day it was. It looked like she was never coming home.

When I did see Aggie coming down the street, I tried to figure out just what I was going to say to her. I tried a couple of things in my mind, but none of them worked. She had a package in her hand. It wasn't much, but I asked her could I carry it for her. She looked at me and didn't say anything. Then she handed me the package. I followed her up the stairs to her apartment and watched as she fished through her bag for the keys and unlocked the door.

"You see him?" she asked after I had sat down.

"No."

"You coming around looking for him here?" she asked.

"I guess so."

"I don't know why you bothering to look for him," she said. "He ain't no damn good."

"He's the coach," I said.

"Oh, stop it!" Aggie put some water on for tea for herself. "You want tea or a beer?"

"I'll take the beer."

"You say he's the coach. He ain't the coach. He's Cal. When you take off the title, that's what he is. Cal. He tell you how we met?"

"Yeah."

"Uh-huh. We met at this party, and he looked at me like I was something good to eat. Ran down the same old line you all use. 'Baby, you so fine.' 'Baby, you this and that.' 'Baby, I need you so much.' Walking around like he was king of the world. Didn't know a blessed thing outside of playing ball, not a blessed thing." Aggie poured the hot water into the teapot, shook the pot once or twice, and put it down on the table. "He wanted to go to bed with me, but he was afraid to ask. Funniest thing in the world. But he was nice and I liked him. The first time I let him stay overnight he took off his clothes and he had his basketball uniform on instead of underwear. I asked him if he was planning on dribbling somewhere.

"We got married and we had the baby and we had

plans. That's the way it comes for poor folk. First
you get the baby and then you look around for the
plan. We got a few dollars in the bank, and he was
talking about buying a house. I got into buying all
those magazines they put out on how to decorate your
house. I was going to have Colonial this and French
Provincial that. The whole thing. Then he got into
trouble, and that was that."

"He told me about the trouble," I said.

"He didn't tell you about the trouble," Aggie said.
"He can tell you what happened, but he can't tell
you about the real trouble because he ain't got that
many words in him. What did he tell you about? The
basketball part?"

"There was more?"

"The basketball part wasn't nothing. He let some
people talk a hole in him. You see all these profes-
sional ballplayers and they got women doing everything for them except sneezing; they got this cat nipping at them and they got that cat nipping at them,
and they don't know what to do. Then they listen to
somebody, and they make a mistake. Then they gone.
It's all over. But that's just the basketball part. That
wasn't nothing because he ended up right back where
we all start out, empty-handed.

"The thing is, most black people don't even realize
they ain't got nothing. They stand on the corner
popping their fingers to some music and figure that's
what it's all about. They figure they ain't supposed
to have nothing. But Cal saw what he could have
had. He saw that he had one thing going for him,
and that was his basketball, and when they cut that

off, they might as well have cut off his manhood right
along with it.

"He couldn't do nothing when it was all over. Only
thing he knew a bed was good for was to lay in with
his eyes open all night. Got so he couldn't stand me.
He would look at me and turn away. That's when I
gave up.

"He had put all them dreams together, and that was
what he had got himself to be, them dreams. When
they died, he was dead, too. He kept his body moving
around, filling it up with alcohol and laying it around
here and there. But it had killed him. He was so damn
busy mourning for himself that he didn't even notice
what was happening to me. Not until our baby died.
You want another beer?"

"Okay."

"You must have caught him just right," she said.
"When he told me he was thinking about getting back
into the game again, I was really surprised. When he
told me that Jack had contacted him, I just held my
breath.

"Who's Jack?"

"Punk. When he got into that trouble in Chicago,
there was this slick dude who went around giving out
money, talking about how he had so many games in
the bag, that kind of thing." Aggie took off her heels
and put on a pair of low dark shoes. She had nice
legs, and she caught me looking at them. I looked
away. "Anyway, this punk had about five or six guys
working for him. One of them was this cat called
Jack. He was trying to be what the white boy was
without the white boy's money."

"He's in New York?" I asked.

"Somewhere," she said. "Cal was over the other night and said that this guy called him and told him things that he figured he had to be connected with what went down in Chicago. He said he was there, so it had to be Jack."

"What he want to mess with Cal for?"

"You know anything about gambling?"

"Yeah," I said. "I can play poker, craps, twenty-one, just about anything."

"Uh-uh." Aggie lit a cigarette, wiped a piece of loose tobacco from her lip with the tip of her finger, and crossed her legs. "These guys who gamble, most of them, aren't about games, or even making money. What they're all about is controlling things. It makes them feel big. They'll spend two, maybe three thousand dollars to pull back one thousand. Then they can call a few of their flunkies and say the fix is in, and everybody thinks they've done something big. They take a woman out they have to show their money off, spend a few hundred dollars, hoping that you'll be impressed. If you are, they're on top of the world; if you're not, their show doesn't work at all.

"This guy, whoever he is, who's trying to deal the bad end of the stick to Cal doesn't care about the money as much as he does about getting to be a big man by controlling, or looking like he was controlling, people. And if Cal crosses him, he's going to be mad because he's going to have to look in the mirror and see himself for what he is—nothing trying to buy into something. Now let me ask you something, you going to sit there and drink up all my beer, or you want to go with me and look around to see if we can get a line on Cal?"

"You know," I said, "this guy Tyrone from the after-hours joint is from Chicago. He's always going back there, too. You don't think he could be this Jack, do you?"

"I'm better at looking than at thinking," Aggie said, smiling.

We went out, and Aggie took me to some places where she thought Cal might be, but it didn't take long to see that she didn't really think he would be at any of them. When I mentioned that to her, she asked me if I thought sitting in the house would be better. I said I didn't know.

"I don't know where you men pick up the myth that a woman's place is always home waiting," she said. "We don't wait at home, ever; it just seems that way. But what you come back to, if you find us there, ain't never what you left. The sooner you get next to that, the sooner you'll make some woman happy."

I nodded and just went on following her around. She seemed more like Mary-Ann than I thought. At first I was thinking it was cool the way Cal and I had picked the same kind of woman, but then it came to me that maybe all women were like them in some way.

Going around with Aggie to the places that she and Cal had been was like seeing a movie of his life. When Aggie talked about the places, telling me little things like what seats they had sat in at the rib joint or how Cal had fallen asleep in a movie, it was like she was remembering something really special to her. All you needed was a drum and maybe a little funky piano in the background, and you could have played what she was saying on the radio, it sounded that good.

"You been to his place?" Aggie asked.

"Yeah, he ain't there," I said.

"I've got a key. Let's look around inside," she said. "You know where it is?"

"Yeah, ain't you been there?"

She shook her head no.

At Cal's apartment Aggie gave me the key. I opened it and went in. Aggie came in and looked around. She looked at everything real slow. At first I thought she had found something when she sat down and stared at a picture. But she was just like going over the past. When she started crying, I wasn't even surprised. She went through some of the stuff on his dresser. It was a mess, really, not much better than I keep my stuff. There was an empty bottle of wine in his closet and a few dollars. I was glad to see the money. Aggie handed me a picture that she had found in Cal's closet. It was a picture of her in an evening gown. It said that she had just released a record.

"How come you ain't still singing?" I asked.

"How come?" Aggie lit up a cigarette, took a deep puff, and let the smoke out slowly between her lips. "Lonnie, I go to sleep at night with 'how come,' and when I wake up in the morning, it's still right there next to me. And you know, I don't mess with it too much because I'm not really sure I want to know 'how come.' Can you get next to that?"

"Yeah," I said.

She shook her head and kept on looking around his

things. I tried thinking about why she didn't want to know more about how come she wasn't singing. It didn't make any sense to me, even though I had said I could understand it.

"You ever get into *Ebony* magazine?" I asked.

"*Ebony*? No, why?"

"You must have been like—the perfect *Ebony* couple, you know. "Sports hero marries famous singer—"

"I wasn't famous, believe me."

"Cal played me one of your records," I said. "Something about a rich woman . . ."

"Hurry home, sweet Daddy," she started to sing.

> An' don't take your time
> If you wait too long
> Your mama will be gone. . . .

She was singing through tears, but the tears took over and she just broke down. I sat there for a minute trying to figure out what to do, and then she snapped out of it, just like that. Wham! One minute mama was messed around and the next she was okay.

"You got straight real quick," I said.

"It's something black women learn," she said. "Let's get out of here."

I took her home, and she asked me to sit with her for a while. She sat and thought, and we made a little small talk. I was sitting on the couch. First she sat at the table; and then she came over and sat with me. She leaned against me, and I put my arm around her. I figured she needed to be with somebody. I held her for a long time, and it was nice. I must have fallen off to sleep after a while. I woke up on the couch, and it was dark. My sneakers were off, and I figured Aggie must have taken them off. Her bedroom door was open, and I went over and saw she was asleep. When I laid back down on the couch, I felt I was guarding her. It was a good feeling.

The next game of the tournament was being held at Mahoney Gym over at City College. Everybody was nervous, even though they didn't want to say anything. Lenny started this thing about who was going to be the coach and stuff, and I sounded on him. What Lenny could do was to play a pretty good game against white cats who didn't play no ball. He couldn't play against no black cats, and he couldn't play against white cats who could play ball because he didn't really have the heart.

When I sounded, Ox said he thought I should be coach, and so did Paul, which blew my mind and Lenny's. I thought Paul would have backed Lenny again.

We didn't have any trouble finding City College, but we had all kinds of trouble finding the gym. When we got there, the place was packed. This fat cat ran up to us as soon as we got there and asked who the coach was, and I said that he'd be a little late and I'd be taking care of things. He said he needed a lineup card right away. I told Lenny to make it out.

"That's supposed to make me feel good?" he said.

I didn't know if it was, but it sure did. My man was grinning and running around like he was a producer or something. There were television cameras there, too. I had seen games at Mahoney on television. Being on the tube was pretty hip. There were a few reporters in the locker room, asking what it meant to us to be exposed to scouts and things like that. I could see that it was getting everybody a little uptight, so I went over and asked the reporters if we could have a few minutes alone. I didn't think they were all going to just leave, but they did, and everybody looked at me to say something. I knew a little about the team we were going to be playing, so I ran that down to them.

"What they got," I said, "is three nice brothers who can bound and this one big white boy named Tomkins who's supposed to be all-world. He's supposed to be going to some big-name college next year. He got that Rick Barry style, passing through the lanes, and he can shoot good from anywhere. Now the thing is, you know if you get near him, the whistle is going to blow. So if you think you're going to foul the sucker, knock the pee out of him so he knows he ain't playing no Mickey Mouses."

"You can hold him, Lonnie," Walter said.

"Right," I said. "But he's going to want to be the star, so if we lock him up right away, he might give us the game. Ox, you fall off if he comes low and help out. Look for the charge."

We went through our warm-ups, and then they told us to sit down. We did, and this cat who announces the Knicks comes out. He introduced a few people, including Sweet Man Johnson, who spoke:

"When I played ball in the streets of New York, I used to dream about playing for the National Basketball Association, of having my name in the papers, of fame and money. I got a lot of my dream. But I got a lot more than I dreamed of. I got the chance to get an education. I got a chance to realize my own potential and to make a contribution to the streets where I had learned my ball. These young men have this same opportunity, and what's more, they have more knowledge of what they're about than I ever did. I would like to take this moment to wish them all the luck in the world, both on and off the court."

There was a lot of applause, and then we had to wait for the television guys to switch the cameras around before we could start. I lined up next to this guy named Tomkins.

"If you try not to get my sneakers dirty," he said, "I won't be too hard on you."

"You must be smoking that oregano, boy," I said to him.

"I like the way you say 'boy'," he said. "You say it like you ain't used to the word."

The ball went up, and Roy got the tap. He tapped it over to Breeze, who waited for everything to settle for a moment before he brought it across court. Roy was on the high post, and Ox had moved low. Paul was starting a circle in the corner. I called for the ball and let Breeze clear to the corner. The play was for Paul to double his man into a pick from the high post. I made like I was going to drive around Tomkins. I put the ball on the floor once, and it was gone. Tomkins had it and was driving downcourt. I went after him. When he slowed down and looked over his shoulder, I knew he saw me. I caught up with him about five feet from the hoop. We went up together, and he slammed on me.

Okay. I got careless. The cat was good. They got the deuce. I brought the ball down, fed it to Ox. Ox took a fall-away jumper, and the ball bounced away from the rim. They got it. I was on Tomkins. He ran down to the high post, turned, got the pass, and shot it behind him to a cat cutting to his right. Another lay-up, another deuce. Everybody was going ape over this cat's pass.

Roy got called for three seconds. Then Ox threw the ball out of bounds. Before I could turn around, they were up ten. We hadn't scored a basket yet. I called time-out.

"You ain't moving, Breeze," Ox said.

"I was open when you threw up that J that didn't touch nothing!"

"We got to box out more on the boards," Roy said. "They boxing me out, and nobody's helping!"

"What's the play, coach?" It was Walter. On the money.

"Let's run the forward picks," I said, patting Walter on the shoulder. "We run it right side, and then we run it left side. We got all the game to get these ten points back," I said. "Let's not throw the game away. We just play it from now on. They need the ten to try to stay even. Let's go."

The first play worked, and we scored. Then they missed, and we came down on the break. Ox blew the cripple, but Roy stuffed the bound. They came back and scored two quick baskets. We scored on a jumper by Roy, and then Ox fouled Tomkins. He hit two, and we brought the ball in. I missed a J, and Tomkins got the bound. He came down and tried to go around me. I just touched the ball, and the whistle blew. He got two shots and made them both.

"Lighten up!" I said to the ref. "I didn't even touch him."

"Watch your mouth!" The ref stood about three feet away from me and stuck his finger in my face. I didn't like that, but I let it slide.

Breeze got tied up, and there was a jump ball. Roy got the tap and passed to me in the corner. I hit the J, and it began to look like a game.

Slowly, but surely, we began to catch up. Then with two minutes to go to the half I came down the right side and drove past Tomkins. They inbounded, and I took the ball away from their center and scored again. They brought the ball down and blew an easy lay-up. I got a good feed from Lenny, who was in the game, and I got to stuff over Tomkins. Ox made another basket, and we went into the locker room with a two-point lead.

We were feeling good, but I told everybody that the game wasn't over yet. We still had another half to go. The half time went quickly, and we were on the court again. This time we got off the first scores. We were up by five points, and we were exchanging basket for basket. First we would be up by seven, then five, then seven, then five again. I began to dig something about Tomkins. When he dribbled with his left hand, he could shoot, and when he dribbled with his right hand, he could pass. But he couldn't switch hands on either. I was all over him, and I took the ball from him twice. I had only picked up one foul in the first half, so I wasn't too worried about that. With six minutes to go and we were up by five, they called time-out and brought in this brother named McDade. He took Tomkins's place, and that made me feel good because I knew he was going out because I smoked him.

The first time I put a move on McDade he just about left his sneakers. I faked right, and that sucker fell over his feet trying to recover when I went around his left side. I made a nice lay-up. Paul dug the action and brought the ball back to me when we got it again. This time I tried to make a move, started around him again, and he almost tore my shirt off. Only they called me for traveling.

They got the ball and got a foul to bring the score down to four points, our favor. Roy tried a short jumper from the outside, and McDade climbed over my back to get it. He was pushing me, elbowing, and just about wrestling me whenever I got near the ball.

I figured I'd have to pick this cat to get free, so I put Ox outside and me inside and ran a forward pick. Only instead of trying to go through the pick, McDade hooked his arm in mine. I pushed him away as hard as I could.

When the whistle blew, I thought it was going to be a foul on McDade, but the ref was calling a technical on me for unsportsmanlike conduct. I couldn't believe it!

"The cat is all over me!" I screamed. "He's pulling my shirt and everything else!"

The referee just looked at me as if I was crazy. I got a towel and wiped my face as McDade blew the technical. Lenny asked me if I wanted to take myself out, and I said no.

They came down, and I backed off McDade, hoping they'd throw him the ball. They did and he started to drive and I went after him. He pulled up real quick and started a jumper from about the foul line. Roy must have went up thirty-five feet in the air and smacked it downcourt. Breeze got the ball, but they recovered, and Roy called a play. He called a right-side screen for Breeze. I rolled left to get out of the way. But when Roy got the ball and tried to pass it to Breeze, they slapped it away. It came to me, and I took it straight in. I started up, and McDade threw his shoulder into my gut.

He fell down on top of me, elbows first, and stayed on me until they got the ball. I put my hand in his face and pushed him off, and the ref called a foul on me.

"What's wrong with you?" I asked.

The ref spun around with his hands in a T. He was calling a second technical foul on me.

"You're *blind,* man!"

"Get off the court!" the ref screamed at me. The vein on his neck was sticking out. "Get off the court!"

Some of the people in the stands started booing, and somebody threw an apple core on the court. Paul had me from the back, and Ox was in front of me, pushing me off the court. Somebody was taking pictures.

They started pushing me towards the locker room.

"Take it easy, man!" It was Sweet Man Johnson. "You're out of the game, so shut up."

"Why should I leave?" I shouted at him. "The cat was all over me. Anybody can see that!"

"Look, the game is over for you," Johnson said. "You either leave now or they'll throw your whole team out of the tournament!"

I went on into the locker room and sat on the bench. I couldn't even think straight. Did he say I was out of the whole game? I had two technicals; I had to be out. I didn't know what was going on. I went to the door of the locker room and looked over to our bench. Johnson was squatting in front of the guys. He was coaching them.

A few minutes later the game was over. The guys came in with their heads down. They got dressed and didn't say nothing. Paul asked me if I was going across town, and I said no. I wanted to be alone. They weren't mad at me, but they didn't want to talk either.

By the time I had finished getting dressed and picking my hair out the gym was just about empty. I went out and saw Johnson standing and talking to a reporter and the guy who had introduced the players. He came over to me.

"Been waiting for you, man."

"Yeah."

"See you ain't got that win stuff in you yet," he said.

"I can win if the ref calls a game like he got at least one good eye," I said.

"Let me tell you something, Lonnie," Johnson said. "There's cats that come into all steps of basketball every year and can't make it. You see little dudes playing ball, and they all pretty good. Then they get to high school, and they find out that some cats can outmuscle them, and the weak cats fall off to the side. They ain't hungry enough to get strong.

"Then they get into college, and they find out some cats are willing to hurt you in order to get over. A lot of guys fall by the wayside because they ain't hungry enough to get hurt.

"Guys come into the pros and find out that everybody in the pros is strong and everybody will put a hurting on you every day of your life. Some of the guys in the pros ain't got nothing near an education. The only thing they can do in life is play ball. You think they're going to let you take that away from them when they know you can't stand no hurting? They're going to hurt you until you know how to protect yourself. And if you blow your cool and throw away your game, they don't care. They getting theirs to beat you, not to look good."

"I guess you're right," I said.

"You know I'm right," Johnson said. "Because you been playing a lot of ball and you see what goes down. That ain't your problem. The problem is that you saw an excuse to lose and you couldn't let it go. It was a hedge, you know. You got to let it go sometime."

"What you talking about?" I looked at him. "Ain't no way I want to lose!"

"No way you want to lose, but you want to hang on to an excuse, just in case," Johnson said. "You were still winning when that guy was on you. Even with him beating on you, you could have won. You found an excuse to blow, and you couldn't let it go. You got to fight through that feeling. You got to make the other team beat you."

I looked at him, and he looked at me. Then he started to get his stuff together and leave.

"Say, Sweet Man?"

He turned around.

"Thanks, man, you're okay."

"Don't sweat it," he said. "Where you are, I've been."

Then he split.

I went to the Grant, and Paul was there.

"Hey."

"Hey," I answered.

"I just wanted to say that you played a nice game," he said.

"I'm going to win next time," I said. "Next time it's to the bust!"

Jimmy Harrison asked me how the game was, and I told him we lost. He said that Paul had told him that the ref was out to get me, and I said no, we just lost.

There was a message for me. Aggie had called. I didn't know if she had been to the game or not. What I was hoping for was that it was something about Cal. I went upstairs and called her, but there wasn't any answer.

I took another shower, and I called her again. Still no answer.

Mary-Ann came over. She asked me about the game, and I had to tell her about it. That was the thing with losing. You had to live with it until you won, and you could never be sure when you were going to win.

When I called Aggie again, she was there. She said that Cal was in jail.

"Jail?" I asked. "What did he do?"

"He got into a fight with some guy and hurt him pretty bad," she said. "I don't even think he wants to get out. I spoke to a bail bondsman, but I don't know if I can raise the money."

"Don't worry about the money," I said. "We'll get it together."

"We can get him out tonight if we can raise three hundred dollars," Aggie said. "We give that to the bondsman, and he'll get Cal out."

"Let me call you back."

I was tired after the game, but after talking to Aggie, I felt more tired than I had ever been in my life.

I fell asleep and must have been sleeping for about an hour when I woke up scared. I jumped up and looked around. I was alone and couldn't figure out why I should be scared. Then someone knocked on the door. It was Mary-Ann.

"I must have been knocking for ten minutes," she said. "Harrison told me you were up here. Tell you the truth I thought Joni was up here with you."

"You hear about Cal?" I asked.

"I heard."

I changed my shirt and started picking out my hair. The only people I knew that could lay their hands on bills that big hung in Ugly's place. I told Mary-Ann I was going over there to borrow the money to get Cal out of jail.

"I'll give you the money," she said in this quiet voice. "If you want it."

I turned and sat on the edge of the dresser. I started to say something about her not to be fooling around, but Mary-Ann wasn't the fooling around type. She took down her jeans. The money was taped to the inside of her leg. She pulled her jeans back up and then brought the money over and put it next to me.

"Where you get all this?" I asked.

"When Paul told me they was trying to raise money to get Cal out of jail, I figured you'd get in on it. So I went back to where we got the letters from . . ."

"Tyrone's?"

She nodded.

I thought about a whole lot of things to say. Things like she shouldn't have done it, and she could have been killed if Tyrone caught her, stuff like that. But the money was laying there, and I needed it, and I took it.

I went over to her and sat next to her on the bed. She put her head against my chest.

"I figure one day, when we laying on our fancy rug, we going to look back on all this and say cool things about it," she said.

"One day that's just what we're going to do," I said. "C'mon over to Aggie's with me. We'll take the money downtown and get some free air for Cal."

"Can't," she said. "Gotta go back over to the club, so Tyrone don't think I did it."

"Ain't you scared?"

"Ain't grits groceries?"

I kissed her again and went over to Aggie's. She had got part of the money from where she worked, and we went downtown to the bondsman. He was a little fat cat with the smallest hands I ever seen on a man.

The fingers weren't even as long as the palm. He counted the money twice, then put it in a drawer. Then he took out his pistol and checked it. I guess that was for my benefit in case I was thinking of taking him off or something. He took out some papers, filled in a few lines, and then me and Aggie went behind him over to the jail.

Cal looked old. Old and mad. Aggie took him by the arm, and he just ignored her. There was a swelling upside his head. He didn't even look black, but kind of grayish.

He didn't say nothing to us, even when we asked him questions, and after a while we didn't say anything to him. The only person who did any talking was the bondsman.

"Anything happen you let me know," he said, "anything at all. He commits suicide or something, the first thing you do is call me. That way you got your money covered."

Cal was like a zombie in the cab and going up the stairs. We got him sat down in the kitchen, and Aggie started serving up some food she had made. Every once in a while she gave me a look, like she didn't know what was going on with him. I didn't know what was going on either. I knew the guy didn't feel good. I been in the slam and I know where that's at.

"What we doing here?" Cal said.

"What you mean?" Aggie asked. "We getting ready to eat."

"This ain't my house," Cal said. "I can't go on playing this game like we're making it and I got a life to be coming home to. I'm tired of playing these games."

"Cal . . ." Aggie tried to put her arms around Cal, and he pushed her away.

Aggie had called Cal's father and he arrived a few minutes after we did. The only time that Cal had mentioned his father was when we were going through his scrapbook. One picture had him standing with a tall guy and I had asked him if that was his coach. He told me that it was his father and he turned the page real quick and I thought that maybe he didn't want to talk about his father because he was dead.

When his father came in, Cal looked at him, shook his head, and turned away. You could tell there wasn't any love lost between them.

His father, whom Aggie called Pop, tried to exchange a few light words with Cal, but Cal wasn't buying. From then on, it was like they were two dogs, each waiting for the other one to make a move and start the fight.

Cal got up and went to the cupboard. There was some rum there and he poured himself a half a water glass and downed it.

"You can't get ready for the big game like that," I said.

"My big games are gone," he said.

"Son." His father started to speak. "These people are—"

"Yes, *dad?*" Cal put the drink down and turned to his father. "What is it, *dad?* Do you have some fatherly advice for your son after all these years?"

In a way I understood about the hurting going on between Cal and his father. When you're little and you get hurt it's bad, because when you're big it's too late to make a comeback. What was bugging Cal was not that his father had done him wrong, but that his father had done wrong to a kid that had later become Cal, and the man couldn't forgive his father for what he had done to that kid. I could understand that.

"Hey, man, do we get to know what happened?" I asked. "I mean, if you just going to be nasty, then we might as well find out what's happening."

"What happened?" Cal poured another glass of rum. Aggie screwed her face up as she watched the glass fill. "What happened was my dear wife smiled at me and brought her warm body up against mine and I forgot everything I ever knew. I forgot about leaving my game somewhere in Chicago. I forgot about all the years in between then and now. Yeah, I forgot.

"But several gentlemen had the kindness to remind me of those things. They came to me and said, 'Nigger, who you think you are?' They said, 'Ain't you that nigger that used to fix ball games in Chicago? We can make some money off you. Yeah, all you got to do is what we tell you.'"

"Oh, Cal!" Aggie slammed her palms down on the table. "Does it ever end?"

"They said they wanted me to do them a little favor." Cal was talking and smiling like he was crazy. "Everybody wants Cal to do them a little favor. O'Donnel wants Cal to do him the favor of dropping out of the tournament so he don't get embarrassed. The gamblers want me to mess with the score so they can make enough chump change to buy somebody else's life. 'If you don't do this for us, we're going to have to make life hard for you,' that what this clown says to me in the car the other night. Then I hit him. I hit him, and hit him, and kept on hitting the sucker until the cops stopped me.

"And then they took me to jail. And I sat in that jail cell, and I had a good laugh. Because that's all I am, is one big dumb JOKE! They beat me in Chicago, and they beat me here. I thought I was Calvin F. Jones. No, man, that ain't who I am. I'm the nigger who sold his game. That's who I am."

"Did you tell the police your side of the story?" I asked. "You tell them your side?"

"Yeah, I told them," Cal said. "One of them said to me, what did he say? Oh, yeah, he said, 'Didn't you used to be Spider Jones?' Ain't that something. 'Didn't you used to be Spider Jones?'"

"We lost yesterday," I said.

"I know."

"You know?" Aggie looked at me.

"The word gets around," Cal said. "Even in the joint. Brothers sitting in there feeling on their dreams like they masturbating. Thinking that one day they're going to come out and sing and dance or play some kind of ball and get on up in the world. What was the name of that book? Yeah, *From Ghetto to Glory*. We like to think that we *are* the ballplayers. That's what we like to think. Truth is, we're more like the ball, giving up our hides to make the game."

"Later for your noise, Cal," I said.

"You don't want to hear this, do you?" Cal looked up at me.

"Why you cutting him up so?" Aggie said. "He's out here busting his butt, trying to get you out of jail, and all you got to do is to cut him up like that?"

"I ain't doing nothing wrong, honey," Cal said. "I just got there with the first knife."

"You ain't coaching the team no more?" I asked.

"It's like this, man—"

"I don't want to hear nothing but are you coaching the team!" I said. "You done sold your game, don't be giving mine away!"

"No," he said.

I went on out the door. Aggie came after me and was talking about how I had to understand. I didn't want to hear it, just like he said.

8

We played our next two games on the same day and without a coach. They were scrub teams that we should have walked on, but we just managed to get by them. I played all right the first game. In the second game, when they found out they were going to lose, they started a lot of crap under the boards. One of their dudes was beating on me every time I got the ball, and I gave him an elbow in the face to keep him off me. When I did that, he grabbed me around the neck and threw me down, and we had a light scuffle on the floor. There were only a few seconds to go, and the referee told both of us to leave the floor. I didn't think nothing of it.

The next day, when I got to the center, Jo-Jo was there. He said a white guy called up and wanted to talk to Cal.

"How you know it was a white guy?" Ox asked.

"He sounded like a white guy," Jo-Jo said. "He said he wanted Cal in his office at ten o'clock Thursday morning, or else!"

"Yeah, he was a white guy," Ox said. "Ain't nobody else is going to be 'or elsing' you on the phone."

I had sworn to God that I would never speak to Cal again. But when the call came, I was anxious to go over and see him. I called over, and Aggie said he wasn't there anymore.

"You mean you don't know where he is again?" I asked.

"I think he's over at his old place," she said.

"You want to come over there with me?"

"No."

"How come?" I asked.

"Here we go with your 'how comes' again," she said. "Well, this time the 'how come' is because I love the man, and I want the man, and the Lord knows I need the man. But I can't go up to him with my heart in a shopping bag and a headful of hope anymore. I just can't make it anymore."

"Look, Aggie." I tried to find the right words. "I ain't a faggot or nothing, but . . . I need Cal. You know what I mean? I don't need him for money or even for ball but . . ."

"How many times you got to be hurt before you know where the pain is coming from?" She spoke as if she might not have been talking to me. "How many times does it take, Lonnie?"

"I don't know, Aggie."

Aggie and I met at the corner of his block. By the time I got there I was doubting Cal myself. We walked up the stairs together and knocked on his door. He didn't answer at first, and when he did, he was so stinking with cheap wine I wanted to throw up. We got some coffee into him and then told him about the phone call.

"I figure it must be O'Donnel," I said. "Jo-Jo wasn't sure."

"All he wants from me is that I don't coach," Cal said. "And I'm not doing that."

"Maybe it's not that," I said. "Johnson's on the road, and maybe he heard we been playing without a coach."

"I don't want nothing from either of you," Cal said. "And there's not a thing I have to give you. So why don't you split?"

"You don't care about me," Aggie said. "Okay, why don't you do it for Lonnie? Or do you want him to get down on his knees and beg? You want me to get down on my knees, Cal? That make you feel better?"

Aggie started to get down on her knees, and Cal caught her and held her up. She looked into his eyes and asked him again if he would show up at O'Donnel's office.

I found myself holding my breath. A memory came to me, something I had never thought about before.

It was me laying on the bed in my room, listening to my mother and father in the kitchen. She was begging him to come back. She was begging him and crying, and I was laying there, holding my breath, waiting for his answer. When he said he couldn't, when he had left and the door was closed and the only sound was Mama's crying in the kitchen, I started hitting the wall with my fist. I hit it and hit it until I couldn't feel the pain anymore.

Aggie wouldn't let Cal look away from her. She made him look her right in the eye. She held his head in her hands and looked him in the face until he stammered that he would go up to O'Donnel's.

"Okay," she said, "okay."

Cal slumped across the bed, and Aggie stood and signaled me towards the door. We went there together and looked back at Cal on the bed. I saw his scrapbook on the floor, and I went back and picked it up and put it on the dresser.

I met Cal in front of O'Donnel's office the next morning. I was there early and waited for him in the lobby. I spoke, but he didn't answer. We got on the elevator and went up to the ninth floor.

O'Donnel's office still impressed me. His secretary smiled at us like she was glad to see us or something. I smiled back, and she took the smile off her face real quick, like the whole thing had been a mistake.

"How you feeling?" I asked Cal as we waited.

"Feeling?" He looked at me. "I'm feeling okay."

"It's a nice day," I said, trying to fill up the space between us.

"Don't worry," he said, "I won't screw anything up for you."

"I wasn't worried, man."

I could smell the liquor on Cal's breath from the night before. I figured O'Donnel would, too. We waited a while longer, and then O'Donnel came out. He took a quick look at us and then went back into his office. A moment later his secretary came over, with that same smile. This time I didn't smile, though.

"Mr. Jones, Mr. O'Donnel would like to see you now," she said. She sounded like somebody making an announcement about a bus being delayed or something. "May I get you a magazine, Mr. Jackson?"

I said okay. Cal went on in, and I sat on the couch wondering what was going on. Now I knew why Mr. O'Donnel's secretary was smiling. Anybody who could chump you off like that, with a smile on their face and making it sound like they were doing you a favor, had to be pleased with themselves.

It seemed like forever that Cal was inside with Mr. O'Donnel. Once Miss Smile went in and I tried to look past her into the office. No way. I couldn't hear anything either. After a while I had to go to the bathroom. I went over and asked Miss Smile if they had one, and she gave me a key and told me to go outside and to the left.

"Second door down," she said, with that same smile on her face and that same voice.

The door didn't say nothing. It was just a blank door, and it was locked. I opened it, and all it was was a bathroom. I couldn't figure why they kept it locked unless they thought somebody was going to steal a free pee or something. But I felt good when I went inside. I went to the toilet; then I washed my hands and put on some of the after-shave lotion they had sitting on the sink and checked myself out in the mirror. Not bad.

I went in, and Cal was still inside with Mr. O'Donnel. I gave Miss Smile the key back, and she gave me another smile. A few minutes later Cal came out.

He didn't say nothing to me. He just started out the door, and I had to hustle to catch up with him. All the way down on the elevator he looked like he didn't even know me.

"He say you couldn't coach?" I asked.

"No," Cal said. "He said you couldn't play!"

The sun was really bright when we hit the street. I didn't know where we were going. Here I had asked Cal to come because I needed him to come and because I thought maybe, if he went, things could work out. Then I ask him what went on with O'Donnel, and he gives me this crappy answer. We went to the train station, and he told me to go on up to the center and wait for him there.

"Why?" I asked.

"Because I got some thinking to do and some phone calls to make," Cal said. "Get the guys together. We got a game at five o'clock tonight."

"We ain't playing until tomorrow," I said.

"We're playing," Cal said, "tonight."

I still didn't know what was going on. Cal acted like he was going to coach. I couldn't figure it.

I went uptown and called around until I got

everybody. I told them we had a game tonight. They were as surprised as I was. But by one o'clock the word was all over the neighborhood. The television company had called the center. Not only were we going to play that night, but we were going to be on television.

"This is how it goes," Cal said as we sat in the center. "There was supposed to be two more games for everybody to determine who the two best teams were, and then they were supposed to play for the championship next Saturday afternoon. But what happened was that the television network dropped a movie, and they're going to run the game on television. So they wanted to make it a championship game, and they picked the two best teams. At least, that's what they said."

"Us and who?" Ox asked.

"Us and Manhattan," Cal said. "What I think it is, is that they want to get Tomkins on television because it's going to look good for the tournament to get a good white player on television."

"Lonnie got him before," Paul said. "Lonnie's going to get him again."

"Yeah." Cal looked away. "You guys meet me here at three. We'll go downtown together."

It was only an hour before we were supposed to meet, and no one really wanted to leave. Some of the guys started drifting out into the center, playing pool or Ping-Pong. I went with them. I didn't think that Cal wanted to talk to me. I was talking to Jo-Jo's sister when Cal called me over.

"What I said earlier was true," Cal said.

"What you said about what?" I asked.

"They don't want you to play." Cal went over and closed the door and locked it. "That's why O'Donnel called me into his office. He said you were already thrown out of one ball game. If you play, we have to forfeit."

I couldn't say anything. I just sat there and looked at him. I didn't know whether to be mad or just break down and cry.

"And what did you say?" I asked.

"All the things you thinking of now," Cal said. "Things like why can't you play? Things like who the hell is this tournament for in the first place? That's what I said. And after I finished saying all that, I looked at him and he looked at me and he said no, that's not how it's going to be."

"And that's that?"

"I asked him could you suit up and sit on the bench if you don't play," Cal said. "And he said it would be okay if you kept your mouth shut during the game. No yelling at referees, no nothing!"

I couldn't even see him through the tears. I didn't want him to see me either. I turned away from him.

"What game did you give away?" I asked. "This ain't no damn game. This is just a lot of crap piled up making itself look like a damn game."

"Look, Lonnie, the game is more than what goes on out on a basketball court. That's just the way we play it, running around in sneakers and bouncing a ball. Everybody plays the game with what they got. Trust me, man."

"Why the hell should I trust you?"

"How about because I need you to? How about that being the best reason to take a chance on me?"

"I trust you," I said. "It ain't your fault."

"Some of it is," Cal said. "But trust me anyway."

"The games they play," Cal said, picking up the phone, "sometimes they forget that anybody can play them once they learn it. And even the losers learn something."

He dialed a number and asked for Jack. I looked up at him, and he looked away. He picked up a Coke that was on the table and drank from it while he waited.

"Who you calling?" I asked.

"Hello, Jack?" He spoke into the phone. "This is Cal. Look, I've been thinking about what you said the other day. Look, man, I don't want any trouble from you. All I want is to get out of this mess, man. . . . Yeah. . . . Yeah. You heard? . . . Yeah, well, we're playing tonight at five o'clock. Uh-huh, it's going to be on channel seven. Yeah. . . . Look, can I get some action on the game someplace?"

I started out of the small room, and Cal grabbed me by the arm. He pushed me back towards a chair.

"Yeah, I think I got a pretty good team," Cal said into the phone receiver. "But I want to put a few dollars the other way. I know everybody thinks we can take them. But what they don't know is that Lonnie has a bad ankle. I'm sitting him out. . . . Yeah, yeah. . . . I got two thousand dollars going. . . . Okay, right."

He hung up.

A thousand thoughts came through my head all at

once. If I couldn't play and the team lost, he was going to make two thousand dollars on us.

"Hey, Cal, the money means that damn much to you?" I asked. "All that talk about throwing away your game, was that just a lot of bull? If this is what you're all about, why don't you go get your wine and find a hole to crawl into?"

"Thought you trusted me, man." Cal looked at me. "Thought we were playing it to the bust this time."

I just sat looking at him, wishing at that minute I had never even seen the dude. Somebody was knocking on the door. I didn't move, and neither did Cal until the knock changed to pounding.

Cal got up, still looking at me, and opened the door. It was Paul. He had Mary-Ann around her waist. At first I thought she was asleep, and then I saw something was the matter with her. Paul put her on the chair, and she almost fell off.

"Mary-Ann! Mary-Ann!" I yelled into her face. She didn't respond. "Mary-Ann!"

"Tyrone," she said, weakly. "Tyrone figured out the money."

"What?" I tried to get closer to her to hear what she was saying.

Cal pushed me to one side and looked into her eyes. Then he took her jacket off and looked at her arms. There was dried blood in the crook of her left arm.

"Get her to the hospital!" Cal said. "It's an OD."

"I'll call for an ambulance," Ox said.

"No time." Cal picked Mary-Ann up in his arms and started for the street. "Flag down a cab!"

We got Mary-Ann into a cab, and Paul and a couple of other women from the club went with her to the hospital.

"I didn't even know she used anything!" I said.

"She probably don't," Cal said. "Somebody gave her a veinful of skag to make it look like she did it herself."

All I could think of was finding Tyrone and killing him. Cal grabbed me and held me and dragged me back to the center. When we got in the clubroom, he threw me against the side of a locker and put his forearm up against my neck and pushed until I thought I was going to pass out.

"Listen to me, fool," he said. "I'm going down the tubes. You can't stop it, and nobody else can. But I'm picking who I'm taking with me and who I'm leaving behind. Now you get your stuff together and get on over to the gym like I told you. Come on, son, please."

I looked at him for a long time, and then I nodded. He stepped back away from me, and I got my stuff from the locker and went on over to the gym.

9

I called the hospital from the Mahoney Gym and found out that Mary-Ann was going to be okay. Everybody was relieved to hear that, and uptight at the same time. I found myself watching every move that Cal made. I told myself that if he pulled something dirty on us, I'd kill him. And for the first time I really meant it.

We got dressed, and Cal told us just to play the best we can. "You go out there and give it everything you got," he said, "and you have to win. Because what you got is more than what they got."

I didn't really want to hear it. A guy came in and

said that there were ten minutes to game time. We all went out, and Cal told me to sit on the bench and put a towel around my legs like I was hurt or something.

"If I ain't going to play, what I got to be here for?" I asked.

"Sit on the bench like I told you," he said. "And look around the stands for cats that look out of place."

"Now what does that mean?" I asked as he walked away.

They interviewed Cal on television. I heard part of it, where they were asking him what the tournament meant to the players. Only they were giving him the answers right along with the questions.

"Besides a chance to be seen by college scouts and, perhaps, a chance to get into a college," the announcer said, "what other benefits does this tournament hold for these fine athletes?"

"For most of them," Cal said, "it's going to end right here. The chances of them making it into college ball are slim at best. It's a fun thing, and that's primarily how it should be looked at."

"Well, of course it's fun," the announcer said, pulling the mike away from Cal, "and though there won't be chances for college ball for all of the players, they will all have had the opportunity to show what they can do."

It went on for a little while longer, but mostly they stayed away from Cal. Then the television guy came over and said that they would be ready in ten minutes. The refs came and told us that, and Cal took us back in the locker room for a final talk.

"Okay, here's the starting five," he said. "Roy in the middle, Paul and Ox up front, Breeze and Jo-Jo in the backcourt. Jo-Jo's going to be on Tomkins. We got to play tough defense and a careful game. No run-and-shoot stuff. Everybody got that?"

"How come Lonnie ain't starting?" Ox asked.

"Because I said so," Cal came back. "Now let's get out there and play some ball."

They all started out but Jo-Jo. He held Cal and me back until everybody had left.

"What's up?" Jo-Jo asked. "You know I can't play with that Tomkins. I want to play real bad, but you got me on their best man, and I know I can't handle the dude."

"I got a reason," Cal said. "Lonnie will tell you all he can about the guy. What I want you to do is just to stop him any way you can. Keep the ball away from him. Hang on him, foul him, get him mad. Just don't let him bust loose. You got something going for you that you didn't have in the first game. You got all these television cameras. He's going to try to look pretty instead of just playing his best. You take that away from him, and you might just get his game. Don't worry about fouls; don't worry about scoring. Just mess with Tomkins. You got that?"

"Yeah." Jo-Jo looked at me, and I gave him a little punch. I told him about how Tomkins shot off his left dribble and passed off his right and everything else I could think about. I told him he could stop him, even though I didn't believe he could.

We went back out, and there was a wall of noise that was unbelievable. Manhattan had a whole cheering section. Joni and her girls looked okay, too, and I was glad for them. The Sweet Man was there, with his shoulder bag on, and he came over and said something to the Manhattan coach; then he said something in passing to Cal. Whatever it was, it made Cal smile.

"What did he say?" I asked.

"Same thing he used to say when we played ball together years ago," Cal said. "Kick their butts!"

The television guys came over and told us to keep the time-outs to a minimum. The game was being taped, so they didn't need them. Then the buzzer went off, and the game started.

The first play of the game went wrong. Roy got the tap and sent it to Jo-Jo. Jo-Jo brought the ball across court, and Tomkins took it from him and went for the lay-up. Jo-Jo tried to stop him and fouled him. We were behind by three, and we were only six seconds into the game.

Cal went up and down the bench, yelling for everybody to play defense.

"Fall back! Fall back!" he shouted.

They scored the first ten points of the game. We finally got on the scoreboard when Ox hit a jumper over Tomkins. But Tomkins brought the ball down and got it right back.

Then Jo-Jo got on Tomkins and started keeping him away from the ball. He got two quick fouls and looked over to the bench. Cal gave him a clenched fist. I looked at Cal, I couldn't believe what he was doing.

"You making Jo-Jo take your weight?" I asked.

"No," Cal said. "You're going to take all of it."

"I sure ain't taking it sitting on the bench," I said.

"There he is, third row," Cal said. "You see him over there?"

I looked over to where Cal was looking and saw Tyrone sitting with Juno and another one of his boys. The other cat had a bandage around his head.

"You do that?" I asked.

"That's right," Cal said. "And if your team can keep the score close, that's going to be some light stuff."

The coach from Manhattan called time-out and complained to the referee that Jo-Jo was mauling Tomkins. The refs told Cal to have Jo-Jo ease up. He called Jo-Jo to the bench and told him to keep up the good work.

The score was 26–18, their favor, and we couldn't seem to get any closer.

"Keep an eye on those guys up there," Cal said.

Paul got hot, and we brought the score within three points. Cal called time-out and got the team over to the bench.

"It's almost half time," Cal said. "I want to go into the locker room either tied or ahead. Go out and get the ball. Take a chance if you have to, but get the ball!"

The whistle blew, and they went back out on the court. It didn't make much sense to me. The refs were blowing the whistle against us so much that half the game seemed to be them on the foul line racking up points. The score was close, but we had so many fouls that they could walk on us in the second half. They inbounded, and the ball went to Tomkins. Jo-Jo had held him to fifteen points, seven of them from the foul line. He was still getting his stuff off, but he was looking raggedy doing it. He came down with the ball and put one of the sweetest moves on Jo-Jo that I had ever seen. He started right and then faked a pass. Jo-Jo went for the fake, and Tomkins got the step. Jo-Jo fouled him as he went by. The whistle blew, and the buzzer sounded from the scorer's bench. We were in a three-for-two situation. Tomkins didn't need it; he hit the first two, and it was half time. We were down by five points.

The locker room was death valley. Everybody was out there playing their hearts out. Paul was playing his best game ever. We were still down by five points, and we had a mountain of fouls against us.

Cal went from guy to guy, saying how good they were playing. Nobody thought that we had a chance. They didn't ask again why I wasn't playing—they knew something was up. When they went out at the beginning of the second half, Tomkins didn't start. They started McDade instead.

"Okay!" Cal said. "Okay!"

"What you 'okaying' for?" I asked. "They just figure that they don't need Tomkins to beat us."

"No, that's not what they're thinking," Cal said. "They're thinking McDade is going to foul out Jo-Jo. They see you sitting here with that towel wrapped around your legs, and they think you can't play. So when McDade fouls Jo-Jo out, Tomkins is going to have a field day. Keep your eyes on those dudes over there, Lonnie. If one of them makes a move, let me know."

McDade came in, and he started playing his raggedy game. He fouled Jo-Jo with an elbow in the mouth.

Jo-Jo was cool and made the basket. Then Breeze intercepted a pass and fed Jo-Jo on the break. Jo-Jo had the step and started up for the shot when McDade tripped him. They called it a nonshooting foul. Cal went up in the air about a foot and a half, then sat back down.

"You ain't going to say nothing?" I asked.

He didn't answer. Jo-Jo was mad and looked towards the bench. He blew the shot, and McDade got the rebound. Jo-Jo went after him and fouled him. He was out of the game.

Cal called Lenny over and told him to go in for Jo-Jo. I was disgusted. Some of the guys were looking over at Cal, but he wouldn't let them catch his eyes.

"One of the dudes with Tyrone just got up," I said.

"This is it," Cal said. "The score is close enough for him to make his bet. He's seen me put Lenny in, and he figures that the spread is going to be just what I told him. Watch the cat that got up; make sure he didn't just go to the bathroom or nothing."

The Manhattan team had put Tomkins back in, and he was doing his thing. He was feeding, hitting from the outside, everything. I didn't see what the guy that went was doing. He went outside of the gym. In the meanwhile, they were beginning to pull away. The lead, which had been down to as little as two points, was back up to twelve two minutes after Tomkins got into the game.

"He's back!" I said.

Cal looked over to where Tyrone was sitting, and Tyrone nodded to him and smiled. I looked at Cal, and he was grinning. It was the biggest damn grin I ever seen in my life.

"He's got his action," Cal said. "And from what I heard in the street it's big action. Now let me tell you something, Lonnie. I'm going to put you in the game, and you got two things you can do. You ready to hear this?"

"I'm ready."

"You can go out there and do nothing and throw away the game," Cal said. "Then Tyrone takes his action, and me and you are just a couple of niggers with our pants down. Or you can go out there and play like you know you can, and we can take this whole thing. We bust Tyrone's action. I can't do it, man, but you can. What you think, you think if I put you in, you can get Spider some class after all these years?"

When I stood up and took my warm-up jacket off, everybody from our neighborhood stood up with me. There was a roar that made even the players on the floor look over to see what was going on. I went over to the bench and reported in for Lenny. O'Donnel was sitting on the end of the bench; his eyes were wide, and he was looking from me to Cal. He called Cal over.

"What's going on?" he said.

"This is a championship game," Cal said. "Don't you think it's time for the champions to start playing?"

I glanced up at the scoreboard. We were down by thirteen. Okay. We had the ball.

"Let's do it!" Paul was shouting. He held up two fingers. I rolled to the right side, ran Tomkins into a pick, and got the ball from Roy. Tomkins had recovered and went up with me. I stuffed over him, and the crowd went crazy.

"I BELIEVE! I BELIEVE!"

Joni was leading the fans on our side of the gym. They had the ball, but all of our guys were alive. Roy knocked a pass away, and Ox scooped it up and flew. He hit a nice reverse lay-up, and the crowd went wild again.

I could feel the game. I could feel everything that was going on. It was as if every player had a string on him and the strings were all tied to me. Anytime anybody moved, I could feel it. I saw everything and knew what everybody was doing. We started coming back. The ball felt good in my hands. When I went up for a shot from the top of the key, it was as if I had never let the ball go, like I was reaching from the top of the key and directing the ball into the hoop.

They put McDade back in, and the first time I went against him he slammed me into the floor. The ball went one way, and I went the other.

Ox ran over to me to grab me before I blew my cool. But I wasn't blowing nothing. I got up and smiled at McDade. No, fool, you don't get my game that easy. You don't get my game and the Spider's game that easy. Not this time around.

I made my shots, and they went down and scored on a back-door play. We tried a break, but they broke it up, knocking the ball to the backcourt. Ox set a pick at midcourt, and I was trying to use it to get across when McDade got me again. This time he ran alongside of me and drove me into the scorer's bench with his hip. I wound up halfway under the bench. The ref gave us the ball but no foul. Yeah. I got up, and McDade was bracing himself. He had his hands up, but I just stepped out of bounds and waited for the ball. I shot a glance over at O'Donnel, and he nodded to me.

Later for you, sucker, I thought.

The next time they got the ball they called time-out and brought Tomkins back in. The score was 81 to 75, their favor. Cal told me to look over at Tyrone. I looked at him, and he was glowering.

I was playing the game of my life. But when Tomkins came back in, he came to *play*. He didn't have the moves, but he had the shot. It was me against him. If I gave him a half an inch to shoot, he'd make the basket. I was coming down on offense, and he was all over me. I had to go up higher on my jumpers, move faster on my drives, concentrate harder at every step. We got the score down to three points, but that's where we stopped. They started matching us basket for basket.

They switched to a tight box and one defense. Tomkins was on me wherever I went. The box was cutting off my drives, and they were boxing out Roy for the bounds. I started to freak a little. I came across the middle, taking cats to one side and then spinning in the air to the other. We closed to within one point, but then Tomkins came down the lane, gave me a shoulder fake, and then went up and stuffed two-handed.

Ox answered that with a soft jumper from the corner that didn't touch nothing but net. They brought the ball into Tomkins. I tapped the ball away from him, and he recovered it. I thought I had lost him, but he backed off, and I realized that he was looking for somebody to pass off to! He passed off and then glanced up at the clock. They were trying to hang on! Tomkins moved without the ball to the corner, and I went with him. A second later the whistle blew. I turned around, and Paul had stolen the ball and called time-out.

"We ain't got time for two shots," Cal said. "There's twenty-eight seconds left, and they got three up on us. We go for the tie. Lonnie, their big man is tired. We got to hope he makes a mistake. You drive on him and try to get the foul."

"No way, man," I said.

"He's tired," Cal said. "A tired man is more likely to foul you. You can do it!"

"That ain't what I mean," I said. "I ain't going for no tie. I'm going for the whole thing."

"You don't have time for two shots," Cal said.

"I got the time," I said. I looked up at the clock. "I got the time."

We brought the ball in, and I went for the drive. I figured it might be easy because they would be thinking about not fouling me. I started my step, and then Tomkins jumped out on me. I was afraid of the charge, so I twisted away from him. The ball came up off the dribble, and I hooked it toward the hoop. It dropped.

They called time-out. I looked up and saw that there were eighteen seconds left.

"They're going to sit on it," Cal said. "We have to foul them as soon as they get the ball. They get the one, and we call time-out and then make a plan for the two. Lonnie, they're going to give Tomkins the ball because he's their best foul shot. As soon as he gets the ball, foul him! You got that?"

They brought the ball in and got it to Tomkins, just like Cal said they would.

"Foul him! Foul him!" I heard Cal screaming from the bench. Tomkins wasn't looking for the shot. He was waiting for the foul. I made a move toward him, and he held up, just turning his back to me. I waited.

"Foul him! Foul him!" Cal was standing on the sideline, screaming.

"Okay!" I yelled. I glanced over at Cal and saw the veins in his neck straining at his shirt collar. But this was my game, too, and this time Cal was going to have to trust me.

I faked to the right and then spun around, reaching in with my left hand. The ball spun away, and I went for it. I got to it a split second before Tomkins did and dribbled it away from him.

"Shoot! Shoot!" They were yelling from the stands. I had the shot for an instant, but I held up.

"Shoot!"

Their center moved into the lane, and Tomkins was back on me. I moved toward the center with Tomkins breathing against the side of my face. I pulled up and put my back to their center. Breeze's man saw me turn with the ball and came to cut off the side away from Tomkins. I brought the ball high over my head for an instant, let them reach, and then passed it over my shoulder to where Breeze should have been. I lost my balance as I let the ball go, and the last thing I saw before I hit the ground was Breeze putting the ball softly against the backboard. The buzzer sounded as I hit the floor.

By the time I got to my feet there were a hundred

hands reaching out and touching me. People were handling me and hugging me. I looked up at the scoreboard. The score read: Manhattan 92–Harlem 91. Then it changed: Harlem 93–Manhattan 92. We had won!

Everybody was screaming and shouting. I felt somebody kissing me on the cheek, and I turned and it was Ox. What the heck, I kissed him back. Some of the guys were trying to lift me to their shoulders, and I felt myself half being lifted, half falling and trying desperately to stay on my feet. Over the heads I could see Cal; he raised a clenched fist, and I gave him one back. Our eyes met over the heads, and it was a great feeling.

Somebody was pulling at my wrist, and I turned and saw that it was one of the television guys. He shouted at me, but I couldn't hear what he was saying. He pointed to the television cameras. They wanted to interview me. I nodded my head yes. I turned to see where Cal was; this was his game as much as mine, maybe more.

When I looked back, I didn't see him at first. When I did, he was headed towards the locker rooms. Right behind him was the bald head of Tyrone, or Jack, or whatever else the creep was calling himself. I struggled to get out of Ox's bear hug and told him to get the police.

"What?" He looked at me again.

"Get the police!" I screamed in his ears.

I fought my way through the crowds. The television guys were interviewing some of the kids, and the rest were clamoring around, mugging for the cameras. I saw the tournament committee setting up the trophies on the side of the room.

It seemed forever before I broke away from the crowd and got to the locker room doors. At the door was the guy with the bandages on his head. I didn't need to be told what was going on inside.

"That your money?" I pointed to the guy's feet.

"Wha' money?" He looked down.

I balled my fist up and used it like a hammer as I smashed the sucker right in the middle of the bandages with everything I could muster. He didn't make a sound. He just grabbed his head, looked up at me for a second as if he was really surprised, and then slowly sunk to the ground. I ran past him into the locker room.

Juno was holding Cal, and Tyrone was punching him in the stomach. Juno had his back to me, and when he turned, it was right into my fist. The pain shot up my arm, and I just knew the hand was busted. Juno turned Cal loose to get at me, and when he did, Cal hit him. Juno fell forward on top of me. He must have weighed a ton. I hit my elbow on a bench and lost all the feeling in my arm. I was trying to push Juno off me when I heard something slam into the lockers. It was Tyrone. Juno got on his feet and headed in the direction of Cal. I thought he was going to tackle Cal, but instead, he went by him towards the door. I made a jump after Juno, and I caught him by the foot. I was on the floor, trying to twist his leg, when I heard a gasp. I turned to look, and Cal was bent over. Tyrone was trying to get away, but Cal was holding one of his hands. Tyrone was punching Cal in the face with the other. Then Cal pushed Tyrone's other hand away, and I saw the knife. He had stabbed Cal!

Tyrone jerked his hand loose and plunged it again into Cal's side. I went to put my hand on the floor to push myself up, and suddenly the side of my head exploded as Juno sent his foot against my jaw.

Juno went out the door and I stumbled after him. I heard screams outside and a shot.

I looked at Cal; he was sitting on the floor against the locker. I pushed myself up and got over to him.

"Don't talk, man," I said. I could see he was hurt bad. "Don't talk . . ."

"You get a win . . . you got to talk about it . . ." Cal said. He was smiling. "It's too sweet to just let it go. Talk to me. How'd it feel?"

"It felt good," I said. The pool of blood was growing, and the bloodstain on his shirt was growing bigger every moment. I put my fingers on it and looked at it. I could hardly see it because I couldn't stop crying.

"Tell me about it, Lonnie," he said. His voice was a whisper. "We got it, didn't we? It was us out there, wasn't it?"

"I knew I couldn't get the shot off," I started, "and when I saw Breeze cut away from . . . Cal, I love you, man. I really do."

"Tell me about the game."

"When I saw Breeze cut away, I didn't know for sure which way he cut, but I . . ."

I felt his body relax as he fell against me. I put my arms around him and tried to explain that I wasn't sure that Breeze would be in the right place, but that

I knew he had taught us that play. And if we did what he had told us, it would work out. And it had.

There were people coming into the locker room. Some of them were police. I felt myself being lifted from the floor. Aggie was bending over Cal; her body was shaking with her crying.

I turned and walked out of the locker room. Outside, the police had Tyrone and Juno and the guy with the bandages.

It didn't seem to matter anymore. I went through the crowd back onto the gym floor. Everything seemed to blend in a jumble of noise and lights. O'Donnel was there, pushing a trophy into my hands; someone was patting me on the back, someone else asking nonsensical questions. I handed the trophy to someone and found an exit.

Five days later, on a sunny morning, Cal was buried. I sat in the second row, behind Cal's pop, and listened to the preacher say things about how Cal had been this and that and how we all had to die sometime. Then there was the long drive out to the cemetery. When we got out there, they didn't put the casket in the ground. They put it under a little tent with flowers all around and said that they were going to put it in the ground later that day. Then we got back into the cars and came back to Harlem.

Hey, I felt so bad leaving him out there. I felt like I was leaving the only friend I had in the world out there. I told Aggie that.

"What else you gonna do, honey?" she said. Her face had all the hurt in it that I felt, and the tears were running down over her mouth.

A week after the funeral Mary-Ann was strong enough to leave the hospital. Coney Island was open again, and I took her out there one morning, early, before the crowds came.

"You hear anything about scholarships?" she asked.

"I got a few letters," I said. "But I'm not worried about it."

"I thought . . ." She started a sentence and didn't finish it. Instead, she just held on tighter to my arm.

"I'm going to try to get into some college, any way I can," I said, answering the question she hadn't asked. "If basketball can get me there, okay. I got to get my game a little better first, though."

"You were Most Valuable Player," Mary-Ann said. "How much better can you get?"

"That ain't the game I'm talking about," I said. "When Cal sent me out on the floor to play, I felt real good. I was telling myself I was getting even with Tyrone and that O'Donnel cat. Whole lot of crap like that was passing through my head. You know what I mean?"

"I think so."

"Well, after the whole deal was down, and Cal got killed, I just went for a long walk. I had my warm-up suit on and the jacket we got. I just walked and walked. And the thing came to me just like Cal was running it. The game was over. I had done my thing on the court, copped a trophy, and I still had to get on with living. Cal said he gave his game away when he sold out to the gamblers. But you know he made a comeback. He had enough of his game left, his all-the-time, off-the-court game, to give some of it to me. I don't even think he knew how real that part of his game was. Maybe 'cause it's harder to deal with. They don't be keeping score so you can check yourself out all the time.

"I figure there are going to be a lot of Tyrones and O'Donnels, you know, good guys and bad guys, that I'm going to have to learn to deal with. I know I can't win all the time, but I got to keep myself in the game, got to keep my game together, so at least I have a chance."

"You think I can get a piece of that game of yours?" Mary-Ann looked up at me.

"You can get a tryout," I said. "I'll check your moves out, mama. See what you got going for yourself."

Mary-Ann smiled just the way I knew she would and held my arm a little tighter. I had a scared feeling in the bottom of my stomach, and a little voice that said, "Hey, maybe you won't make it anyway." I knew that was true, but I also knew I was going to give it my best shot.

There were two kids on the boardwalk. They had a wire trash basket with the bottom beat out tied against the fence and were shooting a basketball through it. They asked me to tie it higher, and I did. They were playing one-on-one, and we watched them for a while. One of the kids missed a shot and kicked the ball. It came my way, and I picked it up.

"Try shooting like this," I said.

I shot and watched the ball bounce off the edge of the basket.

"You don't know nothing about no basketball," the smaller kid said.

He took the ball, and they started to play again.